GOD'S GUNSLINGER

Mexican raiders rode rampant across the south-west in a savage campaign to win back former Mexican territory ceded to the United States. Hezekiah Horn, sheriff of Eden County, Arizona, had both this and a bank robbery to worry about. A former saddle-mate of Hezekiah's, Apache Joe, offered to combine his forces with those of the sheriff. They had a task ahead of them that would test to the limit both their friendship and fighting powers.

DAVE ARMSTRONG

GOD'S GUNSLINGER

Complete and Unabridged

LINFORD
Leicester

First published in Great Britain in 1992 by
Robert Hale Limited
London

First Linford Edition
published 1996
by arrangement with
Robert Hale Limited
London

British Library CIP Data

Armstrong, D. (David), *1953–*
God's gunslinger.—Large print ed.—
Linford western library
1. English fiction—20th century
I. Title II. Series
823.9'14 [F]

ISBN 0–7089–7876–2

Published by
F. A. Thorpe (Publishing) Ltd.
Anstey, Leicestershire

Set by Words & Graphics Ltd.
Anstey, Leicestershire
Printed and bound in Great Britain by
T. J. Press (Padstow) Ltd., Padstow, Cornwall

This book is printed on acid-free paper

1

Wolf Pack

SHERIFF HEZEKIAH HORN had seen the wisp of smoke still rising about a mile away and he knew there was no sense in hurrying the pinto.

When he arrived there he got down a trifle awkwardly off the lean, powerful horse, left leg not as flexible from the knee down as the other. He let the pinto's reins hang down and slowly limped around. The two-room homesteaders' house was a charred ruin and the barn demolished. Whatever horses and cattle had been around had been run off.

As he limped about he suddenly came across the women, the mother and the girl. Their clothes were disarranged in a way that made him scowl.

Their eyes still had a frozen look of horror and the gaping red slash across their throats told how they had finally died.

As he stared at them, the black patch across one eye blank and expressionless, his one good eye, the left, glittered for a moment with silent rage. He kept walking and finally found the man. His corpse was headless. Hezekiah focused his Cyclopean eye on the body. He said aloud, "Big Knife Benito. Probably kept the head to kick around at a campfire. Show what he thinks of the thieving gringos who stole his people's land."

In the barn he found a spade with part of the handle burned away. He dug the graves in the hard earth with effort and sweat and lowered each body in gently. Then he took off his stetson and offered a prayer.

When he got back to the horse he picked up the reins deftly with the hook that had replaced the hand that had been at the end of his right arm. He had got adept at doing things with the curved piece of steel. As he got back on the horse he muttered, "Romero's Raiders came our way. Now we got more than Apaches to worry about."

When he got back to Davenport he rode straight to his office. Tommy Turner, his deputy, looked up as he came in. The little baldheaded man with the long straggly moustache squinted one eye at him. "Well, watcha see? Injuns on the prowl?"

Hezekiah limped across to his desk and sat down. He touched the black-bound book on his desk with the hook. "I just saw something that told me Luis Romero is abroad in the land and, like Jehu in the Good Book, he has the blood of war on his girdle."

The deputy squinted his eyes a little more and shifted the chaw of tobacco from one cheek to the other. He thought of spitting on the floor and then checked himself as he saw the look in Hezekiah's good eye. He said, "As if we ain't got enough trouble with them scalp-huntin' Apaches. That Martindale family okay?"

Hezekiah said flatly, "As dead as Davy Crockett. The mother and girl raped and their throats cut, the father beheaded. My hunch was right. Romero has moved in our direction."

The little deputy swore profanely, face twisted with fury. Hezekiah said, "Cussin' never helped nothin'. We have a mighty dangerous enemy on our hands." He scratched his chin thoughtfully with the hook. "Luis Romero has never forgotten the Treaty of Guadalupe Hidalgo of 1848 and the Gadsen Purchase six years after. They are what gained all those Mexican lands for this United States. Romero thinks both were unjust." He mused, "He was a blueblood, more than a hidalgo, a grandee. His family had estates bigger than you could ride across in a couple of days. He aims to try and get it all back even if he has to stir up all the United States in doing it."

Tommy Turner said, "Looks like

that Big Knife Benito still his chief lootenant."

Hezekiah nodded. "His work, all right, out at the Martindale place."

There was a frantic scratching at a back door. Hezekiah got up and went to open it. A little dog scrambled in, a tiny, delightful, squirming mass of silky hair. Hezekiah bent down and picked him up with his good hand, the dog frantically licking his face with a tongue of affectionate worship.

Hezekiah grinned, "Little Mister Short-tail. You been guardin' the place since I been gone?"

Tommy Turner grunted, "Ain't enough of him to guard nothin'."

Hezekiah put the tiny dog down, pulled out a drawer in his desk and fed him a cookie. Mister Short-tail attacked it with energy.

The deputy said suddenly, "Hey, they's a new gambler come to town. Settled into the Four Aces saloon. Been playin' there a night or two. Looks like he ain't no tinhorn. Classy dresser an

5

talks like a college professer. Name of Myron Merrill." He squinted his eyes again. "But I gotta tell you there's somethin' about him I jest don't fancy. Somethin' sort of — I jest don't know — somethin' in the eyes — "

Hezekiah said evenly, "I better get down and take a look at this jasper later. Meantime I've got to get an entry in the report book about what I've seen today. And let folk here in town know about the Martindales. They were a good family and they had friends."

★ ★ ★

Around about supper time Hezekiah looked across at his deputy. "Well, you comin'?" He appraised the little deputy, a flicker of humour at the corner of his mouth. "I don't know why Emily took on feedin' you as well as me, you ever-hungry critter, but she's done it so let's go call on her."

Tommy Turner looked sarcastically at his boss. "Well, rightly speakin' there's only half of you to feed, the rest of you is blown away. But you have an appetite that could eat a roasted steer sandwiched between two bakeries." Hezekiah grinned. "Just thinkin' of what Emily might have waitin' on her table right now puts an edge on that appetite you're speakin' of."

They closed the office and walked on down the main street, turning about midway down into a side street. They finally opened the front gate to a neat white cottage with a garden in front entirely free of weeds and with a blazing variety of blooms.

Emily Anderson met them at the door. She was a tallish woman, almost matching in height Hezekiah who was not a very big man although lean and hard with a suggestion of muscle that could move into powerful action.

Emily's eyes were wide-spaced, open and kindly. She wore her soft brown hair parted in the middle to end up at the nape of her neck in a full knot of gleaming hair. She had a rich red mouth and below it a cleft in the chin that receded but had a touch of attractive, yielding femininity about it.

She said, looking at the deputy, "So you brought your gluttonous partner with you again, Hezekiah. Seems like instead of eating here we ought to take you both down to my store. Maybe there's enough on the shelves there to keep you both busy."

Tommy Turner swept off his hat, his bald head shining in the lamplight. "Well, now, ma'am, ain't nothin' in that store that can equal what you put on the table before us. You have a touch with vittles that would turn a scrub turkey into somethin' fit for a king."

Emily Anderson smiled. "Come on in, you smooth-talking old flatterer. Let's see if we can really fill you up tonight."

Inside Hezekiah removed his hat. In the closeness of the glowing lamplight his one eye shone blue and clear. His moustache, less long and flamboyant than his deputy's, was starting to grey as was his thinning hair. But somehow there was an air about him of alertness and vigour, anything but that of decreasing energy. He and Tommy Turner looked at the table appreciatively.

There was a great bowl of fatback, that thick strip from the back of a hog, festooned with the crisp green leaves of dandelions; freshly baked biscuits, a plum pie, a jar of blueberry jam and a bowl of rich cream.

Tommy licked his lips. He looked sidewise at the other two. "Am I still gunna git invited here to eat when them weddin' bells ring out for you two?"

Emily said firmly, "As I've told Hezekiah several times, wedding bells will not be ringing for him and me until he takes up a less-hazardous occupation than being a lawman."

Hezekiah cleared his throat. "Now, Emily, I don't figure I ever found anything more hazardous than being a miner. You will recall that I got all these injuries of mine down a mine."

Emily nodded. "Well, that's so but a bullet can do even more damage than that. You only have to receive one in the right place in your job and you are dead." She gave him a steady look. "I was married to a lawman once, remember, and he died trying to apprehend a killer who shot first."

"The time," murmured Hezekiah, "when I let an outlaw do that to me will not come. When I first tried for a lawman's job after that accident in the mine they said I couldn't handle it. Well, I went away and I taught my left hand to do with a gun what my right hand could never do. That's when they took me on."

After they had eaten, the two men heaving satisfied sighs, Hezekiah motioned Tommy to stay in the room.

"You being two-handed, you usually help Emily with the dishes. But I'll do it tonight. I want to talk to her about today."

In the kitchen, hands plunged into the soapy water, Emily faced the sheriff, her gaze grave. "What did you want to tell me?"

Hezekiah slipped the end of his hook through the handle of a cup and hung it neatly in its place. Emily smiled and nodded. Hezekiah's face grew serious. "You heard about what I saw today. It's only the first sign of what could turn into a lot worse. This Romero is a man with a mission to kill every American he sees until he gains mastery of the south-west. He wants to see all this country back under the rule of Mexico. He is a grandee with grand ideas. And what is more he is a guerilla fighter who leads a wolf pack."

Emily was silent. She stared out the window a moment into the darkness. She could see Aram Anderson again as they brought him in, the bullet lodged in his back. She shivered a little and washed another plate clean.

After they had left Emily's house Hezekiah and Tommy Turner went back to the office.

Tommy clumped over and took hold of his beloved scattergun, tucking it under his arm. Hezekiah said mildly, "One day you are going to blast a transgressor with that and they'll be picking him up all over Davenport."

When they went out on the street, Hezekiah now with the little dog at his heels, the sheriff clipped out, "You go south tonight, I'll go north. If there's any trouble, like always fire one shot."

Tommy grunted, "After I've salivated the hombre who started the trouble."

Hezekiah was passing an alley that ran along between two of the stores when Mister Short-tail stopped, hair bristling, and growled. In a flash Hezekiah ducked behind the corner of one building, the little dog scuttling alongside him. He could hear a voice down the alley muttering and the movement of unsteady footsteps.

The sheriff waited, crouched back against the building. A figure came into view. It was lurching a little and waving a pistol in one hand. Hezekiah moved out to where the figure could see him.

The man blinked and began to lift his gun to point it at the sheriff. Hezekiah's gun leapt into his left hand as if catapulted by some unseen force. He had it pointed directly at the other man's chest before the other could bring his own weapon fully upright.

Hezekiah said smoothly, "Now, just who are you gunning for, Charley Hicks?"

"That new feller in town — that Merrill — he cheated me in a card game — "

Hezekiah ruminated, "So he relieved you of most of your poke and you pulled out of the game and drank yourself into this mood, huh?"

The cowboy nodded owlishly. "Thash about the size of it."

Hezekiah surveyed him. "Well, now, you ain't in the best condition to accuse anyone of anything, Charley, but we'll go down and see this Merrill all the same." He moved in the direction of the saloon, the little dog giving two sharp barks and following. Charley Hicks swayed along behind them.

Inside the saloon Hezekiah looked around. He saw his man immediately. The gambler sat at a table down in a corner with his back to a wall. A flicker of a smile creased Hezekiah's face. Men who lived chancy lives never wanted to get shot in the back.

Merrill was fashionably dressed and had the look of someone who had known more genteel surroundings. He was as dark and handsome as a lead actor in a travelling show. His hands were slim and well cared for. They moved in the handling of the cards with the practised ease of an expert pianist playing some difficult étude.

There were several other men in the game, one the sheriff recognised as a successful hotel-keeper in the town, Shane Wartman, a well-dressed, honest man. At sight of one of the other players Hezekiah frowned a little. He was a thin, undersized fellow with a sallow face and shifty eyes called Dick Amiss. It was said he had been involved in several card games when cheating had been involved and he had been put out of them both.

Hezekiah limped up to the table, the little dog at his heels. By now the unsteady figure of Charley Hicks had joined them. Hezekiah looked straight at the gambler. "I'm the sheriff of Eden County and the law in this town of Davenport. Charley Hicks here says you cheated him in a game of cards."

The gambler looked up slowly. His eyes widened a little at sight of a sheriff with one eye and a hook where his right hand should have been. A smile with a touch of mockery in it flitted across his face.

He finished dealing the cards. His voice was mellow, pleasant. "That man standing alongside you, sheriff, is not

15

capable of making any assertion that could be taken seriously."

Hezekiah said softly, "Charley Hicks is an honest man. Not much of a card player. Played a lot of games in this saloon and lost a lot of money here. But this is the first time he ever accused anyone of cheating."

The gambler sat back in his chair. He quietly joined his hands together across his lap. He said evenly, "What do you intend to do about it, sheriff?"

Hezekiah looked around at the other members in the game. Nobody said anything. The sheriff looked back at the gambler. "Don't intend to do anything right now, mister. Ain't no one here backing up Charley. Maybe he saw something they didn't. But I want to tell you right now that if you are ever caught manipulating cards for your dishonest advantage you will go out of this town quicker than a man being chased by a crazy Chinaman with a hatchet."

He turned to go. He looked back

and pointed a finger at Dick Amiss. "And I'd watch who I invite into a game, if I were you. For a few bucks Amiss there would collude with anyone to help cheat someone else."

Amiss shot a venomous look at Hezekiah but the sheriff was limping out of the saloon now, Mister Short-tail giving a bark of defiance, the grumbling Charley Hicks stumbling in the sheriff's wake, mumbling protests.

The gambler took up his hand. He said lightly, "So that's your sheriff? Where's the other half of him? Still, this isn't a very big town, is it?"

He pushed a couple of chips across the table. "What does he keep that dog for — running down buffalo?"

There was silence around the table. Shane Wartman, the well-dressed townsman, carefully took the cheroot out of his mouth. He said drily, "Just one word of advice, Merrill. Don't say anything like that within the sheriff's hearing. It would not be too healthy."

Merrill stared at him. His smile spread to a mocking gleam in his eyes. "Well, well. I must be very sure to steer clear of your dangerous lawman."

2

Slade and the Gambler

THAT evening John Slade came riding into town. He was a tall, solemn-faced man in the early thirties, good-looking in a dark sort of way with a mop of Indian-black hair.

He worked a farm some miles out of town with the same care and attention he paid to everything he did. Slade was the sort of man that Hezekiah had long since noted would be a handy ally in a tight corner. He was one of the first men in town the sheriff would have pinned a deputy's badge on in time of trouble.

John Slade had ridden into town to pay court. The object of his affection was the schoolmarm, Rachel Jones. Rachel was a slender young woman in her mid-thirties whose addiction to her task as a teacher was the main reason she was not married as yet. One look at her with her fine white brow topped by a crown of light brown hair fastidiously groomed, and facial features that would have gained her a job as a model was enough to tell that she must have had beaux a-plenty.

John Slade was not the sort of professional man, doctor or lawyer, who would have been considered most likely to have the front running in a bid for her hand but he was a man who farmed very well.

He had built himself a home that stood strong and roomy on a choice piece of land that was well-watered and grew crops that were the equal of any in the county. The banker Jason Carstairs was the only man who knew the extent of John Slade's savings but he had once confided to a friend that it was a tidy sum, indeed. When John Slade took home a wife she would never want for fancy ribbons for her Sunday bonnet.

Slade rode into the main street

slowly, headed in the direction of the cottage rented by Rachel Jones, but first he stopped his horse at the sheriff's office and dismounted.

As he came in Hezekiah looked up, his good eye flashing a brief sign of welcome. The sheriff never overdid anything.

Slade said casually, "Had a little trouble with some Mex raiders. A couple of 'em tried to run off one or two of my horses. Drove 'em off. Peppered their tails with a little shot."

Hezekiah asked, "You figure a couple of Romero's Raiders?"

"Yeah, wearin' them white shirts and britches. Sombreros big enough to shade an elephant. Bandoliers holding enough to shoot up a whole town slung cross-wise over their shoulders."

Hezekiah stared thoughtfully at the young farmer. "You're in a pretty lonely spot out there, John. If you ever feel like coming into town and hanging around a while — "

Slade said, "If ever I need help to

21

handle a mangy pack of Mex outlaws I'll come into town and take on running a livery or something equally peaceable."

Hezekiah flickered his eyes over the farmer's neat and clean attire. "Come seein' the schoolmarm?"

John Slade nodded. "Yup. It would greatly delight me if that young lady could see her way clear to give up teachin' school to take to being a farmer's wife."

Hezekiah got to his feet. "Time for me and Tommy to take a little walk around the town. Go and do your courting, John."

★ ★ ★

When John Slade left the sheriff's office he made straight for Rachel Jones' cottage. The schoolteacher answered his knock, looking, he thought, as pretty as an ox-eye daisy.

They were a good-looking pair and, as Emily Anderson had commented, together would make a fine couple for any preacher to look upon as he joined them together in holy matrimony.

Rachel had taken Slade inside and they had been talking together for a time when suddenly John Slade said hesitantly, "I hear you've been having another gentleman caller."

Rachel half smiled. "Why, yes. He's only been in town a short while. He called to see me one evening. He's a great reader and he wanted to know if I as the most likely person in town, as he put it, would have a copy of Charles Dickens' *Great Expectations*. Said it's one of his favourite books and he wanted to read it again."

She halted a moment and then, still with the half-smile, continued. "He stayed talking for a while about books. He knows a great deal about them. I found him very pleasant company. I told him he could call again."

John Slade cleared his throat. "Is this — gentleman — a gambler called Merrill?" Rachel stiffened a little. "I don't believe his manner of making a living is important."

Slade said slowly, "No, I guess that maybe ain't important. But gamblers generally ain't noted for being the most honest of men."

Rachel gently corrected, "Are not noted for being the most honest of men." She shook her head with a touch of stubbornness. "I don't really know how honest this gambler is, John, but he is providing me with the most stimulating conversation about literary things I have ever had since I came to this town."

Slade interjected, "Rachel, I don't think you ought — "

The schoolteacher lifted her head defiantly. "John Slade, we have no understanding between us other than that we have found each other's company agreeable. You are free to keep on calling on me if you choose. But let me say I am also free to have Myron Merrill doing the same thing if he wishes to."

John Slade cleared his throat again. Rachel raised her hand. "It's getting late, John. I suggest I get us both a cup of coffee and after that we say goodnight."

Slade watched her going into the kitchen. This was an independent lady sure enough but he felt uneasy about this new association of hers and he knew it wasn't all just jealousy. He wished he'd done more book learning.

* * *

On his nightly prowl Hezekiah found himself in the Four Aces, the little dog at his heels. Mister Short-tail was a common sight on Hezekiah's patrol of the town at night. One or two hands stretched out to pat the little animal as he went past, amused smiles on the faces of some.

Hezekiah had only been in the saloon a couple of minutes when he saw the girl, another new arrival. He blinked his eye a little at the sight.

She wore a beaded frock of a flaming scarlet that would have made a desert sunset look drab. There was a scarlet ribbon about her throat and other pieces threaded through her hair. The brilliant yellow of her hair obviously owed its dazzling shade to a pot of dye. She wore black silk stockings that clung to her shapely legs like the hands of an ardent lover and as she walked her high heels gave her hips a voluptuous quiver. Her wide, full mouth matched the scarlet of her frock and her eyes were a deep lustrous brown. Already men were staring at her with blatant admiration.

But there was one man who looked at her more intently than the others. It was the gambler, Merrill. He made a sign for her to come across to the table at which he was playing. Hezekiah watched closely. He saw the girl note Merrill's gesture and a look almost of disdain came across her face. Then, smiling a little crooked smile, she walked across the room

26

to the gambler, her body a swaying aphrodisiac.

When she reached the gambler he grinned familiarly at her and spoke. The girl answered him, nodding, one hand playing easily at the ribbon about her throat. Through his narrowed eye Hezekiah could see pretty plainly that the two were far from strangers.

After a minute or two the girl moved off from the gambler's table. Almost immediately a man approached her, offering to buy her a drink. The girl looked at him coolly, sized him up and nodded.

Hezekiah seized the opportunity. He limped across and sat down next to Merrill, the little dog trotting alongside him and then lying at his feet.

Idly shuffling the cards with swift, deft fingers, the gambler made no pretence about his non-appreciation of dogs, expecially when brought indoors. He said drily, "I take it your animal is entirely free of fleas, sheriff?"

Hezekiah said easily, "Not absolutely,

although I do my best for him. But I would sooner lie down alongside Mister Short-tail here than with some men I know." Merrill, hands still playing with the cards, smiled. "Does that particularly go for gamblers?"

Hezekiah shook his head. "I got nothin' against gamblers as a whole. Not unless they deal from the bottom of the deck."

Merrill asked blandly, "What card would you like to have dealt to you if you already held a deuce, a three, a four and a five?"

Hezekiah said slowly, "Obviously an ace or a six." The gambler shuffled the deck thoroughly and then made a deft movement. The ace of clubs flashed across the table to Hezekiah, face up, followed the next instant by a six of diamonds. Merrill said softly, "There's your straight with either card." He smiled. "But, mind you, I only do that on rare occasions."

"Like," said Hezekiah steadily, "when you intend to fleece a sucker and you're dealing to yourself?"

Merrill reached across and picked up the two cards he had flicked across to the sheriff. "Riverboat gamblers might do that with those wealthy planters. But I'm just a small-time player matching my skill against that of others who like to play cards for money."

Hezekiah changed the subject. "That girl you were just talking to — who is she?"

Merrill looked at him directly, an amused smile on his lips. "I can see that even your limited sight has revealed her to you as a woman of unusual good looks." He skimmed a few cards across the table and gathered them in again. "Her name is Sheree Brodie. She and I had what you might call an acquaintance in another town at another time. I was surprised to see her turn up here."

Hezekiah ventured. "This going to change your mind about calling on the schoolmarm!"

Merrill's voice froze, his face suddenly

icy. "I don't see what my private affairs have to do with you, Sheriff Horn, but for your information what Sheree Brodie and I had between us is in the past. I have found Rachel Jones to be a most attractive young lady with an excellent mind and a sound knowledge of good literature. I will continue to see her."

Hezekiah said comfortably, "Just askin'. Funny how tangled affairs of the heart can sometimes cause trouble in a town. I aim to have as little trouble in this town as possible."

Merrill murmured, "Noting your certain — ah — physical handicaps, I have no doubt that's how you feel, sheriff."

Hezekiah fixed him steadily with his one eye. It had suddenly attained a steely glint like that at the point of a Bowie knife. The sheriff got up to leave the table. He looked down at the cards in the hands of the gambler. He said conversationally, "You and me are gunna get along fine, gambling man, if you stick to the rules laid down by Mr Edmond Hoyle."

He limped away from the table, the little dog immediately jumping to his feet and following. The gambler's eyes followed the sheriff across the saloon, a growing look of animosity in their poker-faced depths.

The batwing doors had scarcely closed behind Hezekiah when the girl was suddenly alongside him. It was the blonde in the scarlet gown. She touched his arm. Hezekiah turned to face her, his eye fixing her steadily.

The girl's voice was throaty but pleasant. It belied her showy, almost gaudy appearance. She said quickly, "You're Hezekiah Horn. I heard about you in a couple of other towns. You are an honest lawman."

Her eyes suddenly lost the brazen look of anybody's girl. For a moment she was young and tired and searching for some sort of help. Her fingers tightened on his arm. "Look, sheriff, I've seen a lot of towns and a lot of

31

shady saloons. I want to settle down somewhere. Maybe get an honest job, earn money that hasn't come out of some woman-crazy cowhand's pocket. A lot of townspeople don't like saloon girls. They're always looking for a chance to run us out of town."

Her voice was pleading now. "If there's any trouble in the Four Aces it won't come from me, sheriff. Just give me a break and let me see what I can do to get to being something better than a well-dressed floozie."

Hezekiah stared at her, his one eye a disconcerting glittering probe. The girl returned his gaze without flinching. Hezekiah relaxed. He nodded back at the saloon. "You been friends with Merrill before?"

Sheree Brodie gave a crooked grin. "More than friends. But Myron has a habit of taking a lot more than he ever gives." The grin changed to a knowing smile. "I've been in and around this state for nearly a year but this is the first time Myron's ever been in Arizona

Territory. He hasn't heard about you yet." A touch of humour lightened one corner of her mouth. "I don't know why I ask this. Maybe it's just for the times he seemed a better man than he really is. You won't hurt him too bad if he steps out of line, will you?"

Hezekiah gave her a thoughtful look. "All depends if your old flame decides to cross the line. If he stays on the law's side of it, won't be no trouble."

The girl bent down to the little dog to pat it. Mister Short-tail sniffed her hand and then licked it. Hezekiah said, "You just passed the best test I know for being a talker of truth. Don't believe me and Mister Short-tail are gunna have a lot of trouble with you."

He went off into the dark, the little dog again his shadow. The girl smiled after them, something apart from the mascara making her eyes look brighter.

3

Strangers in Town

TOMMY Turner came into the office, eager to say something. Hezekiah blinked his eye at him. "Well, what is it, old man, that you're bustin' to tell me?"

The little deputy burst out, "Coupla queer jiggers just rode in. They is down at Henry Porter's store right now. Idee seems to be they want to buy a new shirt apiece. At least, that's what Henry thinks they mean."

Hezekiah narrowed his eyes. "*Thinks* they mean? Why in tarnation doesn't he *know* what they mean?"

"Ah." Tommy Turner sucked in a breath, delighted at what he was going to say next. "Looks like they are both dummies. Can't talk, neither of them. Looks like they are also brothers."

Hezekiah got to his feet, more interested. "What do you mean — looks like they're brothers?"

Tommy Turner let out a whoop and cackled. "Hezekiah, you jist gotta see 'em. They ain't men — they is mountains. Never seen so much blubber 'cept on a giant hog. But for all that they both look like they gotta lot of muscle beneath the fat. Tell you, I wouldn't fancy gittin' one of those boys riled at me."

He shot an excited grin at the sheriff. "Anyway, Henry wants you to come down and help him out with these dummies. Figured you might know a little about that finger talk they been usin'. They been flyin' it about like their fingers was gunna fly right off their hands."

Hezekiah grumbled, "A little Injun sign language that Apache Joe taught me when we were scouts together is all the finger talk I know. Won't help much with these dummies. But let's go see them, anyway."

When they got to the store and walked inside Hezekiah could hear the raised voice of the storekeeper. It held a note of exasperation, "Now, I don't know exactly what you boys want, how you're gunna pay for it, what in all we're gunna — " His voice trailed off as he saw the sheriff.

Henry Porter was a thin, scrawny man with battered spectacles perched on a bony, buzzard-like beak. He came forward, hands held out pleadingly to the sheriff. "Hezekiah, maybe you can help out here — "

The sheriff switched his gaze to the two men standing facing the owner of the dry goods store. His eye flickered a little as it rested on them. They were immense, two great bears of men, all flesh, rough hair and brute strength. They had two almost identical faces, flat-nosed, thick-lipped and low-browed. The two looked as if they belonged in some long-ago stone age, strangling sabre-toothed tigers with their bare hands.

Their clothes were dirty, tattered and frayed. Obviously they had come to the store to buy a new rig apiece and Henry was having trouble with the purchases.

The two turned their gaze towards Hezekiah. Their eyes were aloof and cold, as if they had lived on the fringe of mankind and were distrusted by men. Hezekiah could understand that. He thought he had better make some move.

He dove his hand into his pocket and pulled out a couple of dollars. He pointed to their pockets with an inquiring look. The men nodded, thrust hands like thick-knuckled clubs into their pockets and each pulled out a handful of money.

Hezekiah said, "Well, you ain't got any trouble about their paying you, Henry. They've been working some place." One of the two, just slightly taller than the fatter one, made an impatient gesture. He walked over to a heap of clothing, picking up a shirt and a pair of pants he might just have been able to struggle into. He motioned to the other man to do the same. Holding the articles in their massive hands, they fronted Henry Porter at his counter, holding out money in their free hands.

Tommy Turned cackled, "See, Henry, nice an' easy, warn't it? You didn't need the sheriff, after all."

The storekeeper, muttering and grumbling, picked the amount of money to pay for the clothes out of the two dirty paws holding it and began to wrap up the items. The fatter giant of the two leered at Hezekiah and made the motion of holding a glass up to his lips and drinking down the contents.

The sheriff murmured, "Wash the trail dust out of the mouth." He pointed out the front window of the store in the direction of the Four Aces saloon. The fat one nodded and the taller one grinned, licking thick lips in anticipation of the whisky.

As the sheriff and Tommy left the store, Hezekiah clipped out at the deputy, "Better keep an eye on those two. Go up to the Four Aces after them. If they get likkered up after what looks like may have been a long dry for them they could do a lot of damage. Either one of them could push the Four Aces over with one hand."

When Tommy Turner came back to the office he was full of further excitement. He burst out, "Here's somethin' for you, sheriff. Them two lee-viathans went right up to the Four Aces and downed four whiskies apiece like they was afraid they was gunna be a ban put on drinkin' the very next minute. They just slid their money over the bar, so no trouble there. But when the barkeep started askin' them questions they couldn't answer they started to git a little riled up. Then about that time that gambler Merrill, he showed up. And you know somethin'?"

The little man's eyes sparkled with

relish at what he was going to say next. "He turned out to be a dab hand at that finger talk. Them two whales, they near fell on his neck with pleasure and there was more fingers workin' overtime than females at a quiltin' party. I heard Merrill say to someone who asked him about it that he once had a deaf mute partner he learned the lingo from. Anyway, he finished up buyin' them two another coupla drinks and sittin' there talkin' with 'em."

He concluded, "Tell you somethin', boss. Them two outsize hombres look like it would take more liquor than Davenport can supply to get them drunk. But I don't figure they've got any idees of goin' on the prod."

Hezekiah screwed up his eye. "Well, not right now maybe. But if ever they did this town would suffer." He sat back in his chair and looked up at the ceiling. He opined, "Strong drink taken in over-large quantities ain't no friend to man." He touched the black-bound volume on his desk with the steel tip of his hook. "The Good Book says, it biteth like a serpent and stingeth like an adder."

Tommy Turner's eyes held a provocative glint. He cackled, "I ain't no Bible-readin' man, like you, Hezekiah, but I do believe the Good Book says somethin' else about likker. It says somewhere, don't it, that it makes glad the heart of man?"

Hezekiah said, "It don't make glad the heart of them that have got to go lookin' for mad dogs all likkered up that go shootin' their pistols off at all and sundry." He went back to his books. "Keep an eye on them, Tommy. It don't seem right that two men that size and with those looks don't pack away inside them a heap of malice that might just break out and do some damage."

It was two days later that Tommy Turner came bustling into the office from a round of the town. "Them two lee-viathans, they both got themselves jobs right here in town. Accordin' to Merrill the gambler, them two is brothers all right. The taller one he calls Big Bart and the other one is Fat Freddie. Seems like that's what they allus been known as." He went on. "Well, looks like Freddie been trained as a blacksmith. Seems he's gunna take over the forge that ole Hector Varden left behind when he died a while ago. The town been needin' a good man to shoe our horseflesh."

Hezekiah prompted, "And the other one?"

Tommy took up his narrative. "Well, him, the one they call Big Bart, seems like he worked for a time as assistant to a wheelwright fixin' an' makin' wagons, buggies, buckboards an' all. Ole Jim Mason said he'd take him on to help him out. Said with shoulders like that he oughta be able to do the liftin' of wheels an' axles that Jim ain't too handy at pickin' up any more."

★ ★ ★

Myron Merrill clicked the little wicket gate behind him and walked up the neat path to Rachel Jones' front door. He was a regular caller now. Rachel met him at the door, smiling.

Merrill stepped inside and took the book from underneath his arm to hand it to her. "It was certainly a pleasure to read it again . . . old Miss Havisham with her decaying bridal feast laid out on the table, Pip with his hopeless love for Estella, Miss Havisham with her undying hate for the man who jilted her, Estella and her fatal marriage — "

He stopped, smiling ruefully. "You know, Miss Jones, that book in a way is full of thwarted romance." He gave her a side-long glance. "I trust your heart is not entirely shut out to the pleasantries of courtship."

Rachel gave him a quick look, smiling a little. "Not entirely, Mr Merrill. I suppose I am as vulnerable to Cupid's dart as the next woman."

"Ah." Merrill was brisk. "Now, isn't it time we stopped this formal Mister and Miss business? Can't it just be Myron and Rachel?"

The girl nodded her head. "Of course. We haven't known each other for long but in a way it seems — "

"Much longer," Merrill finished for her. She nodded again. She said, giving him a kind glance, "And it's good to note that we share the same feelings about helping others. I taught in a special school for deaf mutes for a year or two. I only gave it up when this post here offered itself where I could be a real help to frontier children who otherwise might know no schooling."

Merrill's eyes flickered with a surprise that held the slightest touch of discomfort about it. He laughed.

"And here am I thinking that everything I say to those big overgrown oafs is strictly confidential between them and me."

It was late when he left. John Slade, watching from the back of his horse under some trees some distance away, rode off in a state of black depression.

It looked as if he would need to seek out a different bride to carry across the threshold of his waiting cabin.

★ ★ ★

Tommy Turner swung into the sheriff's office, grumbling aloud. Hezekiah cocked his head. "What's your beef this time, oldtimer?"

The little deputy spluttered, "This here town is bein' invaded by furriners. Couple saddle-tramps rode in today aimin' to hang about for a while until they spend what they were paid off with at the end of a trail drive. Ornery-lookin' customers. Said if they like the place and there's ranch work around might settle down here a while. Tired of travellin' on, they said."

Hezekiah creased his brow above the one eye. "Mebbe so I better look these couple over. The population around here seems to be going up without adding anything of real class to its numbers. Guess I'll find them at the

45

Four Aces or some other saloon."

Hezekiah left the office and sauntered over to the saloon. He picked up the two wandering cowhands Tommy had talked about as soon as he went in. They were standing drinking at the other end of the bar.

Hezekiah ordered his usual sarsaparilla and stood at the bar slowly drinking it and unobtrusively studying the two cowhands. They wore range-battered clothes, no better nor worse than other bunkhouse companions, and they were lean and sun-bitten like all their breed.

But Hezekiah also noted there was a sullen, morose look about them that he had not seen in the faces and eyes of other cowpunchers.

He said conversationally, "You boys spending a time in town?"

One, with heavily-squinted eyes, spoke first. "That's about the size of it, sheriff. We earned our pay hard but now we want to spend it easy."

Hezekiah nodded. "That won't be too hard to do in here. The only way you'd go out of here with more money than when you came in would be if you clubbed the barkeep and robbed the till."

The other cowboy, smaller and a little younger than the other one, grinned fiercely. "Now, that might not be a bad idee if it wasn't you that put it to us, sheriff."

Hezekiah asked, "What are your monikers?" The first cowhand had pulled a sack of tobacco from his pocket and was rolling a smoke. He jerked a thumb. "This here is Hank Smith and I'm Ed Phillips."

Hezekiah fastened his one eye on them. "Well, now, Ed, you and Hank have your fun but don't be too noisy about it. And if you're plannin' on a longer stay there's ranches around that might need hands. But," his eyes fixed them with a Gorgon-like stare, "none of them are lookin' for hands who might leave in the night without thankin' the cook for his tender, loving care."

4

Hezekiah and the Hook

JOHN SLADE rode into town. He
was wearing his Sunday go-to-meeting
suit of black serge, white cotton shirt
and tie of black ribbon. It was the
garb he wore when calling on Rachel
Jones but tonight he was headed for a
different destination.

Riding up the main street, he
dismounted and hitched his horse
outside the Four Aces saloon. Slade
was a man who felt himself to be
crossed in love and he was intent
on finding some degree of solace in
alcohol. Normally a man of solemn
disposition, he was at this time plunged
into a state of depression.

He walked into the saloon, ordered
a bottle and a glass from the barkeep
and sat at a table alone. He started

thinking about the disparities between the gambler Merrill and himself. The man, although he worked at what was generally considered a disreputable trade, had much that John Slade lacked.

Merrill dressed with elegance, had manners to match and in addition was a well-read man. A cloud of despair came over John Slade's thoughts as he pondered upon these things. How could a woman of Rachel Jones' breeding, refinement and education prefer a common dirt-farmer to a well-travelled man of the world who had developed a sense of etiquette and had the knowledge of things that loomed large in a teacher's mind?

He gloomily poured himself a stiff shot of whisky and drank it down. He was getting set to have for himself a drink-sodden evening.

Suddenly a whiff of perfume trickled up his nose and he was aware of a female body right next to him. He looked up and his eyes widened. The girls of the saloon were mostly scrawny or over-weight with a strong touch of the slattern about them.

This one was different. She was dressed in a sky-blue frock with ear-rings and necklace to match. She wore stockings that were a blue-black sheen against the slim curves of her legs and dainty blue slippers encased her equally shapely feet.

Her hair was a mass of blonde waves, expertly tinted, and the startling blue of her eyes was emphasised by delicate touches of the mascara that the other girls usually applied in grotesque blobs. There was a smile about the friendly curve of her mouth. John Slade was too enchanted at the sight of her to notice the faint look of weary distaste at the back of her eyes.

The girl said, "Evening, stranger. Why drink alone when you can have company?"

At that moment as he looked at this houri seemingly conjured up by some incredible genie out of the normal shabby background of the saloon, John Slade's ever-present vision of the elegant Rachel Jones receded a little from his mind. The farmer got awkwardly to his feet. He had never had time for saloon girls before but this one was different.

He blurted, "I'll get another glass from the bar." When he came back the girl was seated at his table as if she belonged there. Once again he missed the glance of mockery at the back of her eyes as she watched the awkward movements of the farmer.

John Slade poured a generous portion of whisky into her glass. The girl murmured, "That will do me for the rest of the evening. Unless, of course, you're planning to get me drunk with something else in mind?"

Slade blushed. He mumbled, "I ain't no woman-hungry cowhand. I'm just pleased to have a little feminine company."

The girl shot a quick look at him, surprised. She took a sip at her drink. She said conversationally, "You a farmer, I guess?"

Slade nodded, a note of enthusiasm coming into his voice. "I got me a farm a few miles out that just can't be beat in Eden County. I worked it up until it's paying me right well. And I've built on it a farmhouse that any woman would find to her taste."

The girl smiled a little at the proud naivete of the farmer. She said lightly, "Then I take it you are an unmarried man looking for a bride?"

At her words a picture of Rachel Jones came flooding back into John Slade's mind. He said unhappily, "I guess so. But don't seem that I'm lucky in love." Sheree Brodie looked at him calculatingly. "You had a lady love turn you down?"

"Sort of." Slade lapsed into silence. The girl said, smiling. "You got a rival?"

John Slade looked up at her thoughtfully. He felt like telling someone. He somehow felt this girl might listen and maybe understand. He began slowly. "You see I ain't had much book learnin'. Folks died when I was young and I had to forget 'bout schoolin' and battle to try to save our farm. Lost that one but I got a job with another farmer and kept saving till I could buy me a little land. I worked that up until I could buy a bigger piece of land and I did the same with it. Then I finally got me the piece of land I have now and it suits me fine."

"So," offered the girl, "you are still a young man, you've got a successful farm and you are looking for a good woman to help you raise a family?"

A slow smile came over the farmer's face. "That is it." The girl went on, "But the girl you had in mind is maybe a bit beyond your reach?"

John Slade nodded, his heart warming towards this girl. "You look to be sort of readin' my mind." He waved his hands a little. "Like I told you, I ain't had no book learnin'. This girl, she's had heaps. And the feller she is taking a shine to is a real dandy. Talks in a fine way and it would appear he has read most everything that them famous writers have written. I jest feel sorta — sorta just like a poor dumb dirt-farmer." He hung his head a little.

The girl's eyes softened. She reached across the table and rested a gentle hand on his arm. "There's no shame in being an honest, hardworking man who has made a success of his profession." Her eyes hardened a little. "Let me tell you, I've had some experience with dandies with soft talk and knowledge of books. One of them treated me really bad one time."

She patted his arm. "Listen, my name's Sheree Brodie. Let's just sit and talk and pretend for a while I'm that girl you seem to have lost. Maybe you haven't lost her, after all." She said emphatically, "All you need do is to bring her attention to the fact that smooth-talking dudes are not always the best choice for a girl."

She looked at him out of the corner of one smiling blue eye. "And maybe if she still doesn't see it your way let her know there's plenty of other pebbles on the beach." She smiled more widely, "And you've met one of those pebbles tonight."

John Slade stared back at her and suddenly a smile creased his dark, solemn face. He was glad he had come to the Four Aces tonight and it had nothing to do with the saloon's liquor supply.

★ ★ ★

Tommy Turner was doing his patrol of his part of the town. The scattergun was cradled under his arm as usual. Now and then in former days when he was more lively he had cracked the butt against the skulls of drunken, noisy nuisances, rarely if ever shooting at anyone.

But today he simply carried the gun out of habit, a threat that he never really put into practice. Still, it looked fearsome and young roisterers respected the peppery little lawman and his weapon.

It was when Tommy had rounded the corner of one of the stores, coming out of a dark alleyway he had wandered down that he heard the footsteps. It was the heavy tread of more than one man — and big men, at that.

He looked around quickly but it was dark and the shadows could have hidden an elephant. He walked on, tensed a little now, aware of the same movement behind him. He stopped suddenly alongside a horse trough. He turned and looked back again. He called, "Hey, who's trackin' me? Come on out and let me see yuh. I got a gun here that can talk mighty loud if you're up to no good."

There was dead silence. Then suddenly there emerged out of the shadows two huge shapes, the deaf mute brothers, Big Bart and Fat Freddie. They were grinning all over their squat, thick-lipped faces, as ugly as some menacing heathen idol.

Tommy peered at them and then relaxed. He thought of what were probably the tiny minds encased in those thick, low-browed skulls and he figured this was the sort of prank that in their infantile way they would think to be funny. He called, "All right, boys, you've had your fun. Now, be on your way." He wished he had the finger talk to make it plain to them.

The two giants came closer to him. They were still grinning but as they drew near Tommy could see there was not a lot of humour in their expressions. There was something in their eyes that spoke of far less jocular intent. A little alarmed, he began to bring the scattergun upright.

But already Big Bart had moved with a speed no onlooker could have thought he possessed. One great splay-fingered hand had closed around the barrel of the gun and wrenched it free of Tommy's grasp as if a baby were holding the other end of it. The giant tossed the gun into the middle of the street.

Tommy spluttered with indignation and began to scuttle after his weapon but already the other giant, Fat Freddie, had grabbed him. The little deputy struggled in the big man's grasp but the hands fastened around him were like the jaws of some mighty steel pincers.

Fat Freddie lifted Tommy in the air, holding him aloft. With one mighty downward movement, he plunged Tommy into the horse-trough, the little man's wildly kicking legs frothing up the water. Fat Freddie released his hold and immediately Big Bart took over.

As the little lawman suddenly surfaced, gasping frantically for breath, Big Bart grabbed him and pushed him under again, holding him down despite the deputy's frenzied struggles.

Big Bart finally dragged Tommy up out of the water, weak and sodden, eyes bulging now, his struggles weaker. Fat

Freddie took over again and once more pushed the deputy under.

Tommy's short legs had stopped kicking now and he rolled over in the trough, weak and half-drowned.

After a while he clawed his way weakly out of the trough. He fell over the side and out, fighting for breath, a saturated wreck, eyes still bulged, his face blue from the near-drowning. He collapsed against the side of the trough and lay there sprawled out for some time.

Then slowly helping himself up against the legs of the trough, he staggered to his feet. When he got upright he reeled over towards his scattergun, bent down to pick it up, almost falling headlong in the effort, and swayed off down the street, heading for the sheriffs office.

Hezekiah mouthed, "What in Hades — "

Tommy said, his voice a weak whisper, "Them two lee-viathans . . . They jumped me and tossed me in a horse trough. They evidently don't like the law — "

Hezekiah's eye gleamed like a diamondback rattlesnake poised to strike. He rapped out, "Get them clothes off and get some blankets around you. We'll start the stove up and you sit by it."

The little deputy protested weakly but Hezekiah was already ripping the clothes off him. In a few minutes Hezekiah had Tommy wrapped in blankets and sitting in front of a warming stove with coffee on the boil. Hezekiah pointed to the stove. "When that coffee boils, pour a mug full and lace it with whisky. And then stay right where you are till I get back."

Hezekiah went out, Mister Short-tail trotting at his heels. When he entered the Four Aces, the little dog still with him, there was a crowd there. Hezekiah spotted the gambler first. He wanted him as an interpreter. He went over to the table and snapped at the gambler,

"Merrill, I want you to come with me right now."

The gambler looked up, a defiant look on his face. "Sheriff, I am in the middle of a game."

Hezekiah said flatly, "Put the cards down and come with me or I'll hammer you across the skull with my Colt right now."

The other men at the table all looked uneasy. One pushed his chair back and moved away.

The gambler narrowed his eyes, opened his mouth to say something and thought better of it. He threw his cards down on the table and got up. He gave the sheriff an ugly glance. "What now, Mr High-and-Mighty Lawman?"

Hezekiah gestured towards where he could see the two giants at the bar, grinning as they drank together. "We are going to ask a question of those two freaks over there. I want you to talk to them for me."

When they reached the bar the two

big brothers turned to face them, still grinning.

"Ask them," said Hezekiah evenly, "if they dumped my deputy in a horse-trough earlier tonight and damn near left him for dead."

A flicker passed over Merrill's face and he flashed his fingers at the two brothers. In reply Big Bart worked his big thick fingers with a flourish. The brothers stood there calmly, confident in their own massive strength, grinning more openly than ever.

A dead quiet had descended on the saloon. Card-players had dropped their cards, drinkers had turned aside from their glasses. Everyone stared at that corner of the bar.

Merrill said coolly, "They say they did what you said they did. They say it was just a big joke."

Big Bart's fingers moved fast again. Hezekiah spoke again, his voice cold and flat. "What did he say that time?"

Merrill grinned. "He said you ought to get a bigger deputy." He looked around expectantly but there was no snigger from anyone in the crowd. Merrill shrugged and kept grinning. Mister Short-tail was sniffing around Big Bart's boots. As he did so he growled.

The giant looked down, lifted one boot casually and kicked the little dog against the bar. Mister Short-tail yelped as his tiny body hit the brass rail.

Hezekiah's hook streaked through the air, a fork of steel lightning. Big Bart stared open-mouthed at his chest and stomach where the hook had torn a long jagged, slash right down through the flesh. The hook stopped at the buckle of his belt.

With one movement, Hezekiah jerked the man towards him and at the same time slipped his own hat off his head with his left hand. As Big Bart was jerked forward at Hezekiah's powerful tug the sheriff slammed the crown of his head into the giant's shocked face, the broken nose instantly pouring blood. Hezekiah released the hook, stood back and kicked the big man in the jaw with the toe of his right boot.

Big Bart, a bleeding ruin, crashed to the floor. Merrill was already sprawling there, knocked down by the force of the sheriff's explosive attack.

Fat Freddie, mouthing incoherent grunts, lumbered at Hezekiah, swinging one leg in a mighty lunging kick. The hook flashed again, sinking into the calf of the lashing leg. Fat Freddie's face twisted with agonising pain. Hezekiah's left hand streaked down to the holster at his hip, coming up with the Colt .44 in his hand. He smashed the barrel against the right side of the giant's head.

There was the sound of breaking bone, the splinters daubed with blood. As the huge man fell backwards there was the ripping sound of flesh as the weight of his body tore Hezekiah's hook free.

Merrill was getting to his feet, stark incredulity on his bulge-eyed face.

Hezekiah pointed the index finger of

his left hand at the gambler. He said, voice stiff with ice, "I do not tolerate unkindness shown to an animal, a small man, a woman or a child. Only cowardly skunks ever hurt them."

He pointed at the two mountainous heaps on the floor. "When those two brainless hulks come around you tell them that if they try anything again like they did tonight I will really hurt them." He turned and limped away, picking up the little dog as he went.

5

Shadows in the Night

HEZEKIAH sat alone in the office in front of the jailhouse as he often did even when there was no one in the cells. Little Mister Short-tail growled before the light tap came at the door, almost the sound of a ghost in the night.

He opened the door and a figure slid past him with the quietness of a wraith risen from the grave. It stood clear of the lamplight in case some late passerby happened to glance in the window. Hezekiah breathed, "Apache Joe — what in Hades — "

The man smiled, showing an array of glittering teeth that would have looked at home in the mouth of a wolf. Mister Short-tail strangely had stopped growling. The shadow bent down to pat him and the little dog licked his hand and went back to where he had been curled up.

The man who had made the entrance was of short stature in the manner of his tribe and had the bow-legs of one almost constantly in the saddle. But there was a quivering alertness about him, a sense of physical strength well above the ordinary, the impression of a lithe-muscled cougar dressed up as a man. He wore the usual head-band of the males of his people, keeping flowing hair out of his eyes, a beaded buckskin shirt, matching trousers and knee-length moccasins obviously made for him by a loving squaw.

He said, "Hola, Hezekiah. How is my old friend, Chief One-eye, the one with the hand of steel?"

Hezekiah stared at him. "You got your nerve Joe, comin' in here like this. Anyone seen you they'd have raised all hell. Probably took a shot at you, too. You Apaches ain't our loving friends — "

The Indian nodded, still smiling. "That is why I came late at night, walking in the shadows." He looked under thick black brows at the lawman. "The memory of Company B and the Indian Scouts is still with you, my friend?"

Hezekiah scowled, "Of course it is, Joe. We had many good rides together until you decided to go back to your tribe and I decided to give up leading the scouts and go mining where I got all this." He gestured to the patch over one eye and the steel claw at the end of his arm.

He went on grimly, "But we ain't riding together these days, Joe — not since you took up that Netdahe life. 'Death to all intruders . . . ' That's what that word means, doesn't it, Joe?"

The Indian nodded his head. Hezekiah pressed on. "And we're the intruders, ain't we, Joe — the Pinda-Lick-O-Ye, the White Eyes, the palefaces?"

Apache Joe stopped smiling. "We

have other intruders. The Nakai-Ye."

Hezekiah said curtly, "The Mexicans? But you've had them longer than you've had us."

The Indian said shortly, "Not this kind. Romero's Riders. They are wolves. They come with gun and knife and they raid us. They wait until our warriors are out on the hunt or riding with a war party and they attack the rancheria. They have raped our women, killed our children — "

Hezekiah stared. "But you are Apaches, great warriors, deadly fighters — "

Apache Joe scowled. "These are not the soft-bellied, cowardly Nakai-Ye we have fought and demolished before. That Romero, he is a demon, a devil, an evil-doer, a snake, a witch — he has nothing but death on his mind. And when men like this have such a purpose they are hard to resist."

Hezekiah fixed him with a long look. "So?"

The Indian returned his gaze steadily. "I have come with an offer, my friend.

It is this. Let us fight together — we Apaches and you, the people of this town and country. Let us conquer these raiders and send them back deep into Mexico where they belong. If this is done, if you will fight with us, I give you my solemn pledge that never again will an Apache make a raid on your Eden County."

Hezekiah thought for a moment. He said sharply, "What does your shaman say about all this? You are the chief but it is the word of the medicine man that counts in the end."

Apache Joe nodded. "That is so. He is one with me in this thought."

Hezekiah snapped, "What about Blue Jacket?"

The Indian shrugged his shoulders, a tight smile creasing his face for a moment. "As with all things, he opposes me. But he is only a sub-chief. I am the true leader."

The sheriff pondered. "He is a dangerous man. One night he will sneak up on you and you will feel

70

the steel in your back."

Apache Joe smiled. "My favourite squaw is the best watch-dog I know. She would skewer him in the doing of it."

Hezekiah thought again. He said pensively, "You have given me a strong thought, my friend. Maybe we can come to terms. Romero's Raiders are the real curse of the south-west. If we can destroy him and you keep your word this part of the territory at least will know peace."

The Indian's brows raised themselves high. "Keep my word? Have you ever known me when I went back on it?"

Hezekiah shook his head. "My apologies, old friend. Not only were you the best tracker I ever had among my scouts but you were the one who never spoke with a crooked tongue." He pursed his lips. "What you ask will be a little difficult to arrange from my end." He shook his head. "My people here still remember your Apache cry — Cat-ra-ra ata un' Innaa n' un' Nakai-Ye!'

71

Death and destruction to all whites and Mexicans . . . "

Apache Joe nodded and smiled. "Inform them that if they fall in with us that cry will no longer include you blancos in this county."

He moved to the door. He glanced back at Hezekiah and a look of affection flashed quickly across his face. "As the Nakai-Ye say, adios. Let's hope that when we meet again it will be in agreement." He vanished through the door like something Hezekiah had only imagined.

The sheriff stared after him. Maybe this bizarre request could work . . .

★ ★ ★

The older one of the two cowpunchers, Ed Phillips, went to the door of the battered cabin and opened it. Myron Merrill stepped in, the two hulking shapes behind him looming up like nightmares out of the dark.

The five men seated themselves

around the room, three on rickety chairs, the two cowpunchers on one of the bunks against one wall.

Phillips growled, "Well, boss, any more movement?"

Merrill spread his hands. "It takes time." He looked around at the other four with a touch of sarcasm on his face. "It takes brains and thought. And all that comes back to me."

The other cowboy, Hank Smith, objected. "Don't pair us up with them two brainless hulks sittin' next yuh."

Big Bart, broken nose now adding further to his grotesque looks, growled like a battered bear. Merrill grinned. "Watch what you say. Big Bart does a little lip-reading." He gestured at the two monsters sitting on the chairs that creaked under their slightest movement. "These two are for muscle power. No matter where we go and what we do they are going to be useful."

He leaned forward and rested his arms on the rickety table he was sitting at. "Now, let me tell you there's plenty of loot in that bank. I made a point of putting in a hefty deposit and the banker has been glad to see me. I've called on him several times and I've learned a lot about their procedures and just where all the money and gold is stashed."

He said reflectively, "He's a nice guy, Jason Carstairs. I just hope we don't have to plug him."

Ed Phillips' face became a cold mask. "I'd plug a dozen bankers to get at their dough."

Merrill snapped, "You've always been trigger-happy, Ed. Good thing that what you've done before has been in other states far removed from Arizona Territory or the sheriff here would know about you. We don't want any trouble until the day we raid the bank. We want everything to go along nice and easy with no suspicion directed at any of us until then. It's got to go right, every step, of the way." He leaned forward. "Now listen . . . " The other four craned

their heads towards him the thought
of the coming coup making them lick
their lips.

★ ★ ★

John Slade had ridden into town again.
He headed for the Four Aces saloon,
hitched his horse outside and went in.
As he did his gaze travelled around the
saloon, looking for the girl. At the same
moment that he saw her she looked
towards him and smiled.

She pointed to an empty table.
Slade nodded and went to the bar
to order drinks. When he reached her
Sheree Brodie gave him a warm look.
"Back again so soon? You must find
something here attractive."

Slade gave her his slow farmer's
smile. "Well, let me tell you it ain't
the liquor. I never did care for it all that
much. And it ain't the card playin'.
That's just a good way of losing money
to some hombre who's had more time
to study it than farmers got time to do.

And it ain't the cowboys who come in here."

He drew a breath. "They smell too much of sweat and cow-muck."

Sheree smiled and her voice dropped a little. She leaned forward impulsively and touched his arm. "Look, I don't believe you've had much to do with saloon girls. We are a funny race. We — we move around a lot. Men know we are only vagrants and so — well, they treat us like that." Her eyes drew his in an honest stare.

John Slade cleared his throat. "Maybe what you're saying is all true. But I don't think a woman has necessarily got to be a housewife to be what you might call a good woman. There's other things."

Sheree smiled wryly. "Like hanging around saloons and encouraging men to drink so the house makes a profit?"

Slade shook his head. "You got me wrong." He gave her a solemn straightforward look. "You look to me like a girl who ain't out to deliberately

76

cheat a man of the money it might have cost him a lot of sweat to earn. I think you are an honest woman. And a mighty good-lookin' one."

Sheree was silent a moment. Then she pointed to the bottle on the table. "Pour me a small one. I don't drink much but what you just said is worth drinking to."

Slade reached for the bottle, his slow smile breaking across his face. It was going to be a pleasant evening.

He had left the saloon later and on an impulse he turned his mount in the direction of Rachel Jones' cottage.

When he got there the light was still on in what he knew to be Rachel's living-room and he could see the outline of two people against the shades. His heart dropping, he stayed, watching.

After a while the front door opened and Merrill came out. Slade heard Rachel's voice saying goodnight and then the gambler came down the path to the front gate.

Slade kneed his horse to move off.

At the sound Merrill turned towards him in a flash. A gun had come up in his hand from a holster at his hip at a speed that made the farmer suck in his breath.

Merrill, tense, poised on the balls of his feet, peered closer. Then suddenly he gave a mocking laugh. "Ah, the displaced lover. I hope you tend your farm better than you court women, Slade. Maybe you just lack the chivalrous touch." The gambler re-holstered his gun in one quick movement and turned to walk back to the main street.

Slade watched him go, face twisted a little with anger. Then he moved his horse back towards the centre of the town.

Passing the sheriff's office he saw a light, hitched his horse and knocked on the door.

Hezekiah opened it. "John Slade, what — ?"

Slade said soberly, "I just ran into Myron Merrill up the road apiece. I surprised him a mite. He pulled a gun on me that fast I could see he acted like a man who's had plenty of trouble and shot his way out of it. Watch him, Hezekiah."

He went back to his horse and rode off.

6

Tangle of Hearts

HEZEKIAH always felt a little cramped in the grey serge suit with the celluloid shirt collar and the black string tie but it was his Sunday go-to-meeting regalia and he donned it each Sabbath.

As he went out on the street from the quiet of Ma Cassidy's respectable boarding house he saw Tommy Turner coming to meet him.

Tommy Turner glared at him. "You got me into this, you — you preacher with a pistol. I don't know iff'n it's worth all this jist to git one of them home-cooked meals later off'n Emily."

Hezekiah allowed a flicker of a smile to pass across his face. "Now, you know, Tommy, that once you get into church and you're standing alongside the Widow Wilson and she's casting them big husband-hungry eyes at you you're gunna start singin' them hymns like a skylark."

Tomy fumed, "Ain't enough that I gotta get dressed up like some dude of a whisky drummer but I gotta face up to that man-dee-vouring woman at the same time. Wore out two husbands already and lookin' for a third."

Hezekiah patted his shoulder. "Gunna make a better man of you, Tommy." Again the smile flickered across his face. "That's if the Widow Wilson don't beat me to it." He walked off, the deputy following, mumbling to himself.

Down at the meeting house Emily Anderson was waiting for them. She was elegant in a blue satin gown and fancy blue bonnet that set her off like a figure stepped out of a frame of something painted by Gainsborough.

Hezekiah looked at her admiringly. "Emily, you look mighty good to me any day but in your Sunday go-to-meetin' clothes you look like — like he groped for words — "like a cactus flower."

Emily smiled. "I'll take that as a compliment, Hezekiah." She looked at the little deputy straggling up behind the sheriff. "I see you're making Tommy do his weekly penance before he comes around with you to eat at my place." Hezekiah grinned. "Tell you truth, Emily, he's coming along right well. Caught him peekin' in my Bible the other day."

The little deputy heard him. He snapped, "Only to see if they is a special punishment in hell for a man who would do this to a feller law officer."

A huge woman with a hawk nose and a gleaming eye suddenly descended upon the deputy. "Thomas Turner, I do declare you are a faithful man. Never a meeting do you miss. I'll be delighted to sit alongside you." She had hold of the little man's arm and was steering him into the chapel before he could protest.

As the other two followed them in Hezekiah murmured against Emily's ear, "His cup runneth over . . ."

★ ★ ★

Later around the abundant table at Emily's place once again the two men sat back, replete, satisfied. Tommy let out a sigh of contentment.

Emily got up from the table, picking up some used plates. Hezekiah joined her in helping clear the table. He said to the deputy, "Go and smoke your pipe or bite on a chaw some place. You're probably too over-loaded to be any help in the kitchen, anyway."

Out in the kitchen, Emily, hands in the wash-up bowl, again looked with an admiring smile at Hezekiah as he expertly slipped the end of his hook through the handle of a cup to hold it while he dried it before slipping it up on its place in the open cupboard. She said, "You do make do a lot better than a lot of men with two hands."

Hezekiah turned to look at her, strong affection in his gaze. "I'd make do a whole lot better if I had you to wife."

Emily looked down at the suds between her fingers. She said pensively, "What do you read in the Good Book about taking a wife, Hezekiah?"

He said instantly, "That Solomon, that old wisehead, he says, 'Whoso findeth a wife findeth a good thing.'" Emily stared out the window. She said quietly, "And whoso findeth a dead husband findeth a bad thing."

"That your only reason for not takin' me up on that offer I am always makin' you — that I'm a lawman who could get shot dead in carryin' out his duty?"

Emily nodded. "My most important reason. But it's a mighty big one, to me, at any rate." Hezekiah cocked his eye at her. "Any other reason?"

Emily turned her gaze fully upon him and looked him over carefully. Hezekiah said roughly, "Well, you ain't lookin' at much — half a man, some say."

Emily was silent a moment. Then she said slowly, "You're not half a man, Hezekiah. A hand and an eye don't count for much. It's a heart and a mind and grit and honesty and a God-fearing outlook that count. You're twice the man of any other I know."

Hezekiah coughed. "In that case, when you gunna say yes?"

Emily picked up another plate to run it through the suds. "When you unpin that star from your chest."

Hezekiah went on drying the dishes. This was a mighty stubborn woman.

★ ★ ★

Slade had ridden in the next morning and met the girl on the boardwalk outside the Four Aces saloon. He said appreciatively, "You sure do look good no matter what you're wearing."

Sheree Brodie looked down at her

prim gingham gown and the no-nonsense shoes she was wearing. She smiled, "Do I fit the picture of an honest, hard-working girl?"

John Slade gave his slow smile. "I figure that the man I am taking you to see will be impressed." He said briskly, "Well, let's get down to Henry Porter's store. I didn't ride in today just to stand here talking to you — nice as that is."

As they entered the store the scrawny little man with the spectacles stared warily at Sheree. He asked in a shrill voice, "This the young-er-lady you told me about, John?" Slade nodded. "Yes, Henry. She's had experience sellin' in stores before."

The storekeeper sniffed, and holding his body, rose a little higher. "Had experience in saloons, too, I hear tell." He looked hard at Sheree. "What do you know about dry goods, miss?"

Sheree looked at him confidently. "Well, now, Mr Porter, what kind of dry goods do you mean?" She started listing off the fabrics, the threads, the ribbons and laces, the men's garments, giving them trade names and the prices they usually sold at.

Henry Porter, eyes widening behind his old spectacles, held up a hand. "I see you're familiar with the goods we sell. But how about getting them off our hands, selling them? You good at that?"

Sheree looked around the store and spotted a woman at the far end. She said, "That lady looks like she might be going to buy a dress. Let me persuade her." In a moment she had left the two men and was approaching the surprised woman with a smile. In a few minutes she had taken a dress off a hook and was wrapping it up for the woman.

Sheree came back to the storekeeper with the money in her hand. She said, "I took the liberty of reducing the article by ten per cent, Mr Porter. It made up her mind for her."

Henry Porter, mouth gaping wide, took the money from her. He said incredulously, "That woman was Marcy Rogers. Spinster. Comes in and looks at everything, handles it, but seldom buys. That's the biggest purchase she's made here in a mule's age."

Slade said, "Looks like you've got yourself a new sales-woman, Henry. Sheree is finished with the saloons and she wants to hold down a job like this."

Henry Porter nodded a still dazed head. "Well, she's got one right here. She can start tomorrow."

As they left the store, Sheree looked at the farmer admiringly. "John Slade, you are no slowcoach farmer. You are a fast worker."

Slade said with a grin, "All depends on what you're selling. You ain't hard to sell, Sheree. Now what we've got to do is get you some lodgings away from that saloon. We'll go see the banker, Jason Carstairs. He and his wife put up people in their home — a school teacher from time to time, once or twice a young lawyer. Got no youngsters of their own and seem to like to give decent young folks a helping hand and to enjoy having them around."

Jason Carstairs was big and fat and genial. His eyes had the steady look about them of a man who was honest and decent from the crown of his balding head to the plump toes filling out his shiny, well-polished boots. He looked at the girl and his face creased into a well-fleshed smile. "So this is Sheree?"

Sheree flashed a glance at Slade. "I've just heard Henry Porter say that. Have you told half the town about me?"

Slade said confidently, "Only a few people who really matter." He looked back at the banker. "Jason, you know I'm not a man to do rash things."

The banker's smile grew deeper. "That you are not, John. You are a young man with an account with us that says a lot about good, sensible, sober living."

Slade nodded. "Well, now, Sheree is fed up with working and living in saloons. Henry Porter is taking her on to work in his store and now she's looking for somewhere to live and eat. She'll pay good board."

Jason Carstairs chuckled. "You know, John, you came at just the right time. Amelia's been like a female cat lately looking for a lost kitten. Seems like she'd dearly love to see another young face around our home again. And for that matter, so would I." He chuckled again, looking at Sheree. "And that's a face that would bring cheer to any home. Go round and see Amelia. She'll fix that young lady up with a room right away."

When they left the banker, Sheree stared at the farmer. "This is incredible. And all through your coming into the Four Aces one night and telling me you guessed you had lost the girl you really loved."

A quick shadow passed over the farmer's face. The girl took note of it.

She touched his arm gently. "Maybe we can do something together to make up for that." She slipped her hand into his. "Let's go get a cup of coffee some place. I'll pay. You've done enough for me today." Slade protested but then smiled and nodded. They went off up the main street together.

★ ★ ★

Later that day in the afternoon the gambler Merrill was talking together in front of the blacksmith's forge with the giant brother called Fat Freddie.

A graceful figure came down the boardwalk towards them holding a dainty parasol over her head. It was Rachel Jones, the schoolteacher, having just dismissed her classes for the day. Merrill saw her coming and swung aside, sweeping his hat from his well-brushed head.

Rachel stopped, smiling. She nodded at the sweating and grimy giant, great chest bared showing hair like the pelt of a grizzly. She said to Merrill, "This obviously is one of those brothers you told me about."

Merrill nodded. "Yes. I do what I can to help them."

Fat Freddie was staring at Rachel, eyes running greedily over her finely curved feminine form. A great tongue pushed itself out between his lips and began to roam around them lasciviously. His fingers worked rapidly as he passed a comment to Merrill on them.

Rachel's eyes widened in shocked disbelief. A crimson flush swept up from her throat to her cheeks. She said almost incoherently, "Why, that's — that's disgusting — "

Merrill, eyes blazing with sudden rage, turned on the giant, his own fingers working like fury. Fat Freddie's eyes held a glint of alarm at what the gambler was saying to him. He backed off, with another sidelong silent leer at the schoolteacher, and disappeared into the forge.

Merrill turned to Rachel, all swift apology. "You must do your best to overlook that. It won't happen again. These two brothers, I am afraid, have lived pretty rough lives, some of it quite disreputable. The women they have encountered have usually been of a low type."

He darted a quick baleful look into the forge. "And what's more, of course, he didn't realise you can read the sign language."

Rachel was recovering herself a little, her flush beginning to recede. "I — I didn't realise men made those sort of comments about women's bodies." Her face registered extreme distaste. "And being made by a deaf mute it seemed doubly ugly — "

Merrill took her arm, all gentle consideration. "Come along, I'll see you home." He looked back at the forge angrily. "And I'll see you are never insulted in that way again." He said, with a touch of upright asperity, "I'm afraid these two are good workmen but they have a lot to learn about gallantry towards ladies."

Mollified a little, Rachel let him take her arm. But as they continued on up the boardwalk she looked back at the forge and a slight shudder of repugnance passed through her.

* * *

Merrill later that night found himself back in the Four Aces, the thought of the incident between Rachel and Fat Freddie still rankling in his mind. He thought savagely, I'll have to keep those two on a tighter leash. They could have all the women they wanted after the bank raid and the money was theirs and they were free of the town.

But until then it was good policy for all his group to be taken for law-abiding, honest, morally decent men.

There was no one at his table but there was a crowd gathering at a table a little further off.

The main centre of attraction in the

game being played was a young ranch hand, a boy with the face of a cherub and a mop of curls to match. His eyes were alight with excitement and he let out a whoop as he scooped his further winnings across the table.

An older cowhand grunted, "Young Lonnie Purvis of the Rocking Z has struck a lucky streak tonight. That's the most he's ever cleaned up in his young life."

Merrill strolled over and watched the game for a while. The boy swooped on further winnings, whooping again as he did so. Merrill shook his head. If the kid had been playing at his table he would have soon brought his streak to an end. But then, he thought sardonically, here the boy must have been in an honest game.

He turned and walked away. He had more things to do than watching some dumb kid win at cards — things like planning further for the raid on the bank.

Another man stood on the fringe

of the crowd around the table. He was a nondescript character, looking a mixture of breeds with Mexican or Indian dominating. His eyes looked sleepy but in actuality they were darting everywhere, noting every item about the boy's winnings, totting it all up in the mind.

Later, the game ended, the excited and happy Lonnie Purvis began to gather all his winnings together.

A voice called, "Hey, Lonnie, you riding out alone to the Rocking Z tonight with all that money? Better stay in town till tomorrow, kid."

The boy flashed a grin. "You talkin' 'bout bushwhackers? Man, I got me a rifle and a sixgun. Anyone tries to rob me gunna get a slug where it hurts most. Anyway, ain't no Raiders or Apaches around right now. Ain't seen hide nor hair on 'em for a week or two."

The man of the mixed breeds who had been watching silently slipped away. When he got outside he swung aboard his horse and galloped off in a flurry of hoofbeats. Inside the saloon the grinning boy was just preparing to leave, pockets bulging with his loot . . .

* * *

It was midway through the next morning when Tommy Turner came stomping into the sheriff's office, face grim.

Hezekiah, about to leave on another errand, stopped halfway across the room, staring at the deputy.

Tommy burst out, "Didn't get far in that ride to scout out what's happenin' at Apache Joe's rancheria. Found Lonnie Purvis. Lyin' there, robbed of every cent he won last night at the Four Aces. Throat cut from ear to ear. Big Knife Benito, you bet."

Hezekiah ruminated, "Must have had some spy in here yesterday, lookin' out the strength of the town. Saw the kid and his winnings and let the Raiders know." He frowned. "That 'breed that runs that little goat farm out of town could be their man. Needs watching."

7

Hezekiah Holed Up

HEZEKIAH finished filling up the saddlebags and let them hang down. His rifle was already in the boot, belts of ammunition of .44 slugs to fit both rifle and Colt revolver strapped around his waist and slung across each shoulder.

He swung himself up on to the back of his pinto, Pete. He looked down at Tommy Turner affectionately. "Just keep that blunderbuss of yours handy and make sure there ain't no trouble in the town. I'll be gone just maybe a day or two."

He kneed the pinto and rode off, Tommy Turner shaking his head as he watched. But, thought the deputy, once the sheriff made up his mind he followed his course of action like a hound trailing an escaped prisoner.

As he turned Tommy almost bumped into Myron Merrill coming along the boardwalk. The gambler waved a hand in the direction of the departing Hezekiah. "The sheriff looks to have a little business on hand. Well armed for it, too, it seems."

Tommy spat into the street again. He growled, "He's gone out scoutin' up them Mexican raiders. Figgers that if he finds out a little more about where they are an' what they is up to it'll give him a better chance of protectin' the people of this town — includin' no-account gamblers and their dummy friends." He spat again and went on into the sheriff's office.

Merrill grinned coldly at the deputy's back and then gázed thoughtfully after the vanishing sheriff. He speeded up his walk and moved quickly out to the edge of town. When he came to the dilapidated shanty he went in without knocking. Ed Phillips and Hank Smith raised their heads from the table where they had been emptying two plates of bacon and beans and two steaming cups of coffee.

Merrill said urgently, "I've just seen the sheriff heading out on a reconnaissance trip, hunting on his own signs of those Mexican raiders." His eyes gleamed. "I want you two boys to fork your broncs right now and trail him. Somewhere up a gulch out there you can catch him up and let him have a slug in the back. Everyone will think it was the raiders. Or maybe the Apaches."

Ed Phillips blinked for a moment and then a cold-eyed grin spread across his face. "Gotcha, boss. This will be a pleasure." Hank Smith was already getting to his feet, a reflection of the other man's grin on his own thin-lipped face.

After an hour's ride Hezekiah found himself in the mountains, the great gaping barrancas, the canyons, opening up before him. The pinto was sure-footed moving across the rock-strewn ground that more and more looked like dangerous marbles the devil himself had tossed in their way. They came suddenly to a canyon that looked a little more hospitable than the others.

As Hezekiah rode cautiously into the canyon, easing the rifle a little out of its scabbard, he saw that the cliff face on either side was pitted with caves, a number of which could provide shelter for a group of men. The sheriff drew the pinto to a halt, got down and began walking up the cliff face on one side towards what looked the most likely caves to be used, rifle now in hand.

It was in the third cave he entered that he saw the heap at one end. He limped closer. It was a big supply of food and ammunition. He had found at least one lair of the raiders.

The sheriff rode out of the canyon. He had found a good deal of what he wanted to know. As the pinto picked his way between the devilish rocks Hezekiah suddenly saw the horsemen approaching him in the distance. If he rode on he would meet them headlong. He turned the pinto to his right, heading up another canyon that might lead him around the oncoming riders.

Behind him he heard a faint cry. He had been seen by the other horsemen. He urged the pinto on. And then he saw his mistake, He was in a box canyon, closed at the far end.

He kneed the horse on, dismounted, and led the pinto behind some rocks out of the line of fire. He walked back and got behind a boulder he could see around. He levelled his rifle across it, holding the barrel in line with the hook, lining up the sights with his good left eye.

The following horsemen came into view. They were Mexicans, all right, big sombreros, cartridge-belts crossed over shoulders, saddles ornamented with silver.

There were six of them. They slid off their horses like lightning when they caught the glint off the barrel of Hezekiah's rifle but one was not quick enough. He finished his slide from the saddle with blood splashing his chest where the sheriff's slug had torn its bloody way through the flesh.

Five left, thought Hezekiah. Wish I had Tommy here with his scattergun.

The raiders had raced for cover, rifles in hand. Next moment a fusillade of shots hummed over Hezekiah's head, one or two ricocheting off the boulder in front of him. He ducked down and then came up quickly and let off a couple of rounds in quick reply. As he ducked his head back again he saw that two of the raiders, scuttling behind rocks, had drawn a little closer to him. It would be hard to keep the whole five of them pinned down. He kept on firing, hoping he could figure out something.

* * *

Back on the trail Hezekiah had taken, Ed Phillips and Hank Smith had lost the sheriff's tracks. Not used to the maze of canyons and ravines studded with fearsome rocks that Hezekiah knew so well, they were wandering, at a loss.

Ed Phillips reined in his horse, cursing. "Ain't no good. That one-armed sheriff's just plumb disappeared."

Hank Smith said tightly, "We got company."

Ed Phillips spun his head around. To their right he saw the group of figures on horseback. They had long hair with head-bands to keep it out of their eyes, wore kabuns or thigh-length moccasins and armas or soft calf-leather skirts protecting the riders' legs and feet and the belly of their horses from high cacti and prickly brush. They were mounted on ponies that looked as if they could out-run a deer.

In their lead was a rider in the blue jacket with gold buttons of an officer in the U.S. cavalry, obviously scalped to obtain it.

Ed Phillips rasped, "Apaches — better

run for it — " He swung his horse around and dug his heels into its flanks. Hank Smith followed at a gallop, both men now crouched over their mounts' necks to provide a smaller target.

Behind them Blue Jacket waved his arm and screeched at his riders to follow. In a moment they were racing after the two white men, ponies at the full gallop, the riders' hair streaming in the wind.

Suddenly Ed Phillips' horse stumbled over a rock and half fell. Hank Smith, without looking to either side, swept past him. Cursing, Ed Phillips jerked his horse's head up and whipped it on. But the stumble had enabled the Apaches to get within range.

A bronco buck threw a carbine to his shoulder and fired. Phillips slumped in the saddle and fell. His body dropped and hit the ground, one foot still entangled in the stirrup. The horse, frightened, galloped on madly, dragging the man's bouncing body for a few yards. Then the dead man's foot came loose and the horse galloped on without him. Phillips lying on the trail with a bloody hole between his shoulder blades.

The Apaches pulled up for a moment and the one who had fired the shot leapt from his mount, scalping knife ready. As he remounted, scalp in hand, the others cheered wildly.

By now Hank Smith had stretched out a long lead and was whipping his horse on frantically. Blue Jacket threw his hand aloft and pulled up his riders. No sense in chasing a man they couldn't catch until they were on the verge of the town he was heading for.

The little group turned and headed back the way they had come, jubilant. They had gone out hunting and were delighted to have picked up on the way the scalp of one of the hated Pinda-Lick-O-Ye, a detested White-Eye.

★ ★ ★

Back in the box canyon where he was holed up Hezekiah was blazing away at his besiegers, still managing to hold them off.

Another raider had shown a little too much of himself and Hezekiah, looking through the sight of the rifle, had picked him off with precise accuracy.

The man now lay sprawled on his back, gazing up at the sky with wide-open eyes that saw nothing any more. But the others were persistent in drawing closer, their fire keeping Hezekiah pinned down while his own fire could not hope to keep them back much longer.

Behind Hezekiah the pinto had come up a little closer, as if anxious about the fate of his master. Hezekiah peered around his rock and saw one of the raiders trying to draw a bead on the horse. Unmounted, the sheriff would have had absolutely no hope of escape.

Hezekiah lined up the marksman and had the satisfaction of hearing the man screech with pain. He caught a faint glimpse of the raider vanishing from sight, left eye almost torn out by the sliver that Hezekiah's shot had driven from the rock the raider crouched behind.

Hezekiah waved to the horse to go back. Pinto Pete, ever obedient to his master, ambled back out of sight. The wound the sheriff had given the raider brought an answering hail of lead from the others.

Hezekiah looked back at the pinto and wondered about the chances of getting to the horse and re-mounting. But then where would he go? The canyon was blocked off at that end and if he rode forward he would be cut down in a storm of lead.

Out of the corner of his eye he saw another raider scuttle from behind a rock to another one that brought him almost side-on to the sheriff.

Hezekiah thought grimly. He would now have to answer fire from two very different directions and, what was more, that man's new position had

Hezekiah's body much more exposed to him. As if to prove it the raider who had made the advance let off a shot at the sheriff that almost hit the rifle held in Hezekiah's grasp. He heard the man's yell and high-pitched laugh. The sheriff wondered how many of them he could pick off before they moved in on him in a final onslaught.

And then suddenly the raider who was the farthest back from Hezekiah let out a warning yell. "Mansos! Mansos!" The sheriff sat up, pricking his ears. That was a Spanish name for the Apaches given them long ago by a Jesuit priest.

Suddenly he saw the four raiders, one moaning and holding his eye, running from their cover. They were heading for their horses in a hurry. Next moment they were wheeling their horses, mounted in a flash, to race out of the canyon. As they galloped out the entrance and turned their mounts to race headlong from the place a group of Apaches came into view, heading after the Mexicans, whooping and yelling.

Hezekiah stood and watched. He breathed out loud, "Apache Joe in the lead — how in Hades — "

He limped back, calling the horse. As the pinto came up, whinnying, Hezekiah patted him and climbed on board. As he rode out of the canyon riders were coming back towards him.

Apache Joe was in front. The chief rode up, his leathery face creased in a grin, holding up his arm in a salute. "Greetings, Chief One-eye. Looks like we picked a good time to ride by. Those Nakai-Ye had you pretty near buffaloed in there." He looked over at the two dead bodies lying where Hezekiah's slugs had put them. "Although seems they didn't have it all their way." His grin deepened. "That other four sure were keen to live to fight another day. Running after them would have been like chasing a jack-rabbit on foot."

The bronco braves with the chief did not share his smiling recognition of the sheriff. They were looking at Hezekiah with the baleful stare they gave to all the blancos, the White-Eyes, but not daring to make a move contrary to their chiefs wishes. Hezekiah looked keenly at Apache Joe.

"How come you just happened to be in this here vicinity?"

The Indian kept smiling. "We've got a couple of hunting parties out. Need some meat for the rancheria. Blue Jacket's heading another party. Lucky we were on the scene, huh?"

Hezekiah nodded. "I owe you, Joe."

The chief nodded back, his eyes gleaming. "You sure do. Does this clinch that bargain I tried to make with you that night I called on you in your town?"

Hezekiah looked thoughtful. He said slowly, "I guess it does, chief. Although some of my townspeople ain't gunna take too kindly to it."

Apache Joe smiled. "Well, we'll leave it to you to fix that side of it, Hezekiah. But we can take it the deal is made?"

Hezekiah nodded. There was the

sound of swift approaching hoofbeats. He turned his head quickly. From another direction another group of head-banded warriors appeared, their leader Blue Jacket. The sub-chief rode up, glaring at Hezekiah. He looked at Apache Joe and started to jabber at him in an angry staccato, stabbing a fierce stare at the sheriff.

Apache Joe, smile replaced by a black frown, growled at the other Indian, eyes glittering with anger. Blue Jacket kept protesting, riding his horse insultingly up alongside the sheriff, almost jostling Pinto Pete. The pinto whinnied, shaking his head.

Apache Joe was now snarling at Blue Jacket. The sub-chief finally stopped his barrage of protest and turned back to join his own group, warriors whom he could evidently call his own followers. Looking back at Apache Joe, eyes blazing, he spat straight in the direction of Hezekiah and then, wheeling his horse, he led his band off at a gallop back along the way they had come.

Apache Joe, still smouldering with rage, snarled, "That Blue Jacket . . . Wanted to know why I didn't take your head. Said he and his group saw you ride in here and were going to trail you when they ran across two other whites. They chased them and scalped one and were coming back for you when they found I had caught up with you."

Hezekiah said drily, "I got the gist of it. If he'd-a known you also saved me from them Mex raiders I guess he woulda choked on his own spit." He mused, "Two other white riders in here, huh? Wonder what they mighta been lookin' for? Seems like one of them ain't never gunna find it."

He gestured after Blue Jacket. "You figure you can keep that fire-eater in line?"

Apache Joe's face hardened. "That I'll do even if I have to put my knife in his heart." He turned to his warriors and raised his arm. They moved off, the chief giving Hezekiah one final wave. The sheriff turned Pinto Pete's head back to Davenport.

★ ★ ★

Later, back in the town, Myron Merrill finished talking with a white-faced Hank Smith recently dismounted from a hard-breathing, sweat-soaked horse. All the luck seemed to be going the law's way.

Well, he thought, viciously, that was all going to change the day they took every last cent out of that bank.

8

The Stick-up

MERILL looked around at the other three, Hank Smith and the two man-mountain brothers. He said sharply, "Well, now there's only four of us. Losing Ed lost us a handy gun and a man who's pulled off jobs like this before. But now we've got to do it with one man less."

He stood up from his chair in the ramshackle cabin. He said pointedly, "We've got to get every detail right. First, we've got to try to make sure that one-eyed sheriff and his deputy are not around. If there's no reason for them to be out of town on the day, we've got to make one for them."

Hank Smith offered, "They're gettin' kinda concerned about the safety of farmers and their families in the county now that them raiders are movin' around so much. Hear tell they burned down another farmhouse the other day and slit a couple more throats. The sheriff and his depitty will be riding out to the farms more often."

Merrill nodded. "Well, we've got to make our strike while they're doing it." He took a couple of paces across the loose boards of the floor and turned back to face them all. The same time he spoke aloud to Smith he was also flashing his fingers for the mutes.

"We'll move in well after noon. That's a quiet time in the bank when the whole town's having a sort of siesta. There's two tellers as well as the banker and a skinny old book-keeper who works out back. None of them ought to be much trouble, although I hear tell there was a raid on this bank by some drifters a few years ago and the banker Carstairs showed some spunk."

Hank Smith agreed. "Yeah. I hear

he foiled the raid and winged one of the drifters. He's a man it might just take a slug to stop."

Merrill said slowly, "We don't want any shooting if we can avoid it. But if it's going to take a bullet to stop him, he's going to get it." The brute faces of Big Bart and Fat Freddie brightened up at the thought of hurting someone. Merrill went on: "Freddie will wait out the back with the horses. Hank, you'll take care of the tellers. Bart will attend to the book-keeper and I'll personally see to Jason Carstairs. We'll get the tellers to open the safes and they'll hand over the cash and gold. Hank and Bart will give them a hand to make it quicker." He looked at Bart and flashed a message to him on his fingers, saying it aloud for Smith. "I'm looking to you to put your man out of action very quickly."

Bart grinned, something approximating to the snarl of a wolf sighting a lame deer. Merrill added, "Carstairs won't get a chance to wing one of us. If he tries it, his company will be looking for a new banker."

Hank Smith spoke up. "Hey, that saloon girl you used to know one time, that Sheree, she's been boardin' with Carstairs and his wife ever since she gave up workin' at the Four Aces and took up that job in that store. Maybe she could be a help, livin' with the Carstairs and knowin' somethin' of what the banker's up to. Maybe — "

Merrill cut in. "I've thought about it. If Sheree could see it our way we could cut her in on a share." He stroked his chin reminiscently, a gleam in his eyes. "She was some girl. I had some high times with her. Even thought of taking up with her again but I dumped her once in St Louis and took up with a fancy Creole, and she doesn't remember that too kindly. I think we'd better just go ahead with it the way we've planned and leave the thinking about women until after it's done."

★ ★ ★

Hezekiah and Tommy Turner jogged along, the farmhouse just coming into sight. Tommy sniffed appreciatively as he surveyed a waving crop. "That's them Coopers, all right. Sodbusters that sure know what they're doin'. Everything about their place looks good and healthy — crops, cows, horses, chickens. Be a bad thing to see them raiders put a torch to it."

Hezekiah grunted, "Guess that's what we're out here tryin' to see they don't do."

There was a man ploughing in a field on their left. They swung their horses over towards him. As they drew near he whoa-ed the plough horse and walked over to them. Tommy called, "Howdy, Nathan." The farmer nodded. "What brings you two law officers out this way?"

Hezekiah eased himself in the saddle. "Seen anything of them Mex raiders, Nathan?" The farmer shook his head.

"Nary a sign, Hezekiah. Don't mean they ain't around, though."

Herekiah was emphatic. "Dang right. They are around and they are a bloody bunch. Feller called Luis Romero headin' them up. Figures he can win back for Mexico the land they lost to the United States. An' one way he figures he can do it is to wipe out all the gringos he comes across. Watch out for your family, Nathan."

Tommy Turner added, "Anytime you might feel you may be in real danger, Nathan, Hezekiah says you better pack up an' skedaddle into town."

The farmer looked disturbed. "Well, now that's some problem. I got good crops comin' on an' I gotta git 'em in. Can't let 'em jest rot in the ground. An' there is stock to be fed and watered — "

Hezekiah cut in, "Best save the lives of your family before all else, Nathan. Anyway, think about it. We can't do much for you while you're out here.

But if things start to look real bad best forgit about your crops and bring your stock into Davenport with your family until we can call a halt to these killer raids."

The farmer shook his head. "A mite easier said than done, sheriff, but I'll sure bear what you said in mind."

As they turned their horses away, Tommy muttered to the sheriff, "That feller got two of the prettiest young daughters in the county. Hate to see them raiders git their hands on them."

Hezekiah clipped out, "We can't make them come in, deputy. If they want to hold on out here not much we can do about it."

They had ridden in another direction for half an hour when they saw the small group approaching. As they drew closer Hezekiah said shortly, "That's young Luther Schultz riding in front of the wagon. Looks like old Herman drivin' the wagon with Heidi alongside him — " He and Tommy moved their horses to meet the group.

The young man on the saddle horse saluted them. He was big, full of the German bulk and strength of his parents in the wagon but he had a smoke-blackened face and his clothes were singed and burnt. Before the lawmen could speak he burst out, "Raiders, sheriff. Run off our stock. Left our farmhouse and barn burnin' down when they rode off. We finally drove them off but were lucky to do it." The muscles of his jaw knotted. "Killed ole gramps. Granny's in the back of the wagon with a bad leg. Got a slug in it."

Hezekiah clipped, "Romero's Mexicans?" The young man said bitterly, "They wasn't Christy's Minstrels, that's for sure. Would have cut our throats if they'd got inside the house. But maybe they wanted the stock for meat more than they wanted us. Mighta thought too, the flames an smoke would get us, anyway."

Hezekiah bit out, "We'll get back with you into town in case they are still around. Gotta get that old lady to the doc." He turned his horse. He was thinking, Romero has got to be a big problem.

* * *

Back in Davenport the four riders had gone around to the back of the bank. Three dismounted, leaving one huge fat man in charge of the horses and the pack mule.

Merrill said briskly, "We'll go in the back way." They forced their way through the door. The first person they saw was the old book-keeper, scrawny and pale-faced, sitting on the high stool. He turned a startled face towards them.

Big Bart lunged across the room and smashed the barrel of his Colt across the old man's head. The man fell from the stool like a puppet disengaged from its strings, eyes closed and a bloody wound where the giant had hit him.

They moved on into the bank proper.

The two tellers spun around at the noise behind them to find themselves looking down the barrels of three pistols. The tellers backed off, white-faced. Merrill handed them the canvas sacks he had in his hand. He said, his voice deadly, "Open those safes and put everything in there into these bags." Hank and Big Bart prodded the men with their guns as the two tellers, sweating with fright, moved to obey.

There was only one customer on the other side of the tellers' cages, a middle-aged woman staring at them with eyes as big as an owl's with fright. Merrill whipped around her side of the counter. He said silkily, "Don't move, lady, and you'll live." The woman stood fixed to the spot as if a great magnet held her there.

The tellers were opening the safes, fingers fumbling with fright, keeping an apprehensive eye on the guns. Suddenly a door opened and Jason Carstairs appeared, staring at the scene in disbelief. The banker turned quickly back into his office, slamming the door behind him.

Hank Smith's gun went off. The cowboy was blinking nervously, one side of his face twitching. His shot had smashed a small hole in the door, splintering the wood. There was a heavy thud from the other side of the door.

Merrill snapped, "Keep an eye on this woman" and moved quickly to the slammed door, wrenching it open. Inside the banker was sprawled face down on the floor, a hole in his back oozing blood. He had never reached the desk in which Merrill knew there would have been a weapon. The gambler thought, the banker had spunk, all right, but it hadn't done him much good this time.

He went back into the other part of the bank where the tellers were now terrifiedly shovelling money and gold into the sacks he had given them. He glared at Smith, "We could have done without that, cowboy." He glanced over at the woman. She had fainted and was crumpled up on the floor.

Merrill gestured at Hank Smith. "Help them get that money into those sacks. I'll keep the pistol on them." The cowboy moved jerkily towards the safes, Big Bart already helping to drag out their contents.

As they finished emptying the safes, running footsteps and voices sounded outside. Merrill gestured to the back door and they ran out through it. They pushed the canvas sacks into the saddlebags on the pack mule and, leaping on their mounts, whipped them into action. Fat Freddie dragged the pack mule alongside him at a gallop.

Behind them there were yells and shouting. Once a stray bullet passed over their heads from someone who carried a side-arm. But then they were gone out of sight up the main street, heading for the mountains . . .

They had slowed down now, picking their way through the fierce rubble of the canyon of savage rock. Hank muttered to Merrill, "You sure this is the shortest way to Mexico?"

Merrill said curtly, "I've been through this country before. It's the devil's playground and it stretches from here all the way east clear over to Texas. It's the Badlands and no one hurries through it. It will slow up any posse after us and they'll be hard put to find the trail and know just what canyons we passed through."

The two mutes sat on their horses, stone-faced, indifferent to the hard travelling but eyes flickering every now and again with a look of greed to the pack mule loaded with provisions and with their golden haul.

Smith complained, "You didn't give me a straight answer."

Merrill snapped, "It's the quickest way to Sonora because it's the hardest way and the best way to cover up our trail. Now, let's stop jawing and keep travelling."

Hank Smith sank into the sort of silence that was natural to the two mutes. They rode on for another hour or two, the horses gingerly moving across the rock-stubbled ground until shadows started to fall.

Merrill said suddenly, "We'll make camp here." The two giants slid off their horses with pleased looks as he gave them the sign, Hank Smith dismounting in surly acquiescence. The cowboy would have preferred riding night hawk on an unruly herd to travelling across country like this but he could see they had no choice, Merrill knowing how to thread their way for them through the canyons.

As he unsaddled his horse, Smith was wondering what had brought Merrill through this sort of country before, whether it was here in Arizona Territory or as far over as Texas. Probably, he thought, fleeing some lawman. It seemed like Merrill had been a rascal in many sorts of ways.

The gambler had set them to take guard in turn and it was when it was

Fat Freddie's turn that Merrill found a great paw placed over his mouth and woke up to find the giant kneeling alongside him, eyes gleaming a warning in the dark.

Merrill sat up quickly and the fat man's fingers flashed off a message. Merrill grunted, "Riders in the night, probably sneaking up on us — " He got to his feet, grabbing up the rifle by his side and thankful that the big man's affliction didn't extend to his ears and eyes.

The giant led him back to the point he had been watching from, moving quickly and silently for all his bulk, and jabbed a thick finger into the darkness.

Merrill could see the dim outline of horses tethered down the entrance to the canyon and he could pick up an odd figure or two flitting from one piece of cover to another as they came closer.

Merrill tried a shot. One figure jumped behind a rock, cursing aloud in

Spanish, Merrill snapped, "Mex raiders — they'll try to kill us just for the heck of it — "

Hank Smith and Big Bart came stumbling up out of their blankets, grabbing up their rifles as they came.

Merrill said briskly, "Spread out." He motioned Freddie to start shooting from where he was and Big Bart to go out to the left of his brother. He said against Hank Smith's ear, "Line up next to Freddie. I'll take the right flank." Then he was gone, crouching low as he scuttled across the ground.

Firing from the raiders had already broken out. Merrill, listening to the sound and knowing that it was a heavy hail of bullets figured quickly that there must be at least a dozen raiders out there. He thought, that's mighty poor odds for us — three to one. He pumped a few shots in the direction of the raiders and ducked down again. He called to the others, "Keep firing. Give 'em hell. We'll drive those greasers off."

He was moving backwards as he spoke, ducking behind one rocky spur after another, firing shot after shot as he went. Reaching the spot, he scuttled down to where he had used his saddle for a pillow. He grabbed up the saddle and ran quickly to where they had left their horses. Behind him he could hear the three he had left keeping up their fire.

Quickly he saddled his mount and rounded up the pack-mule tethered closer to where they had been sleeping, the saddlebags still hanging from its back. Dragging the pack-mule behind him, he set the two animals off at a gallop for the other end of the canyon.

Hank Smith heard the sound of the hoofbeats and gathered what was happening. In a sudden rage he stood up, yelling at Merrill, and fired a shot after him. Almost as soon as the cowboy stood erect a raider's slug took him in the back. Hank Smith tumbled over, never to spend his share of the haul from the bank.

The raiders began to make a rush, scrambling over the rocks. A man in the lead with big black moustaches, the bandy legs of a former vaquero, and with a frantic gleam in the eyes of a man afflicted with mania sanguinis, a mad lust for blood, reached Big Bart first. But the giant was staring sightlessly into the night, a neat hole through his head just above the nose. The ex-vaquero cursed, waving vainly the knife almost as long as a sword he carried in one hand.

Fat Freddie had got up and was lumbering as fast as he could towards where his horse was tethered with the others. The man with the knife took after him, his bandy legs carrying him at a surprising speed.

As he felt the man gaining on him, Freddie turned and fired a desperate shot. It flew over his pursuer's head. As Freddie turned and fired he stumbled and fell. The man chasing him was on him like a jaguar coming down from a rocky ledge on top of a deer.

Freddie turned a frantic face upwards but already Big Knife Benito's weapon was slicing deep into his throat.

9

The Chase

MERILL was making the best progress he could over the rocky floor of the canyon, dragging the pack-mule alongside. But he could hear behind him the hoofbeats of the raiders still coming, evidently intent on catching up with him and finishing their bloody work.

When his own mount and the mule both stumbled once more and almost fell Merrill pulled both animals to a halt. He slid off his horse and went quickly to the side of the mule. Moving with the utmost speed, he transferred the banknotes and the gold from the mule's saddlebags to his own. He had to toss away some of his provisions to make room for the loot.

He left the provisions in the mule's

135

saddlebags because there was no room in his own for them and he did not want his pursuers to have any suspicion that the mule might have been carrying anything other than food. He grimaced and hoped there would be enough game on the trail to add to his scanty provisions.

He remounted his horse and drove it on fast, leaving the mule behind. He couldn't hope to make the best time over this terrain but he knew that the raiders would also be slowed down. He hoped they would settle for the mule. If he kept riding on through the night they would probably tire of the chase.

★ ★ ★

Back in Davenport Hezekiah faced one of the bank tellers, his eyes narrowed down to a hard slit. He held up the hook for the man to slow down. He said, "Tell it to me quiet-like."

The man recounted all the details of the stick-up. Hezekiah listened, eye gleaming. He broke in, "Who was it killed Jason?"

The teller jabbered, "The skinny guy. Looked like a cowpuncher. Shot him in the back. Jason must have been going back for a gun."

Hezekiah said, "Uh-huh. That was one of the best men this town ever saw. We'll get them for this if we have to chase them down to the South Pole. That's if them Mex raiders or the Apache under that crazy Blue Jacket don't get them first."

He jerked out at Tommy, "We gotta get a posse together. And don't forget your scattergun. Blastin' that skinny cowpoke with it ought to be right to your fancy."

He moved out of the bank and went along to the doctor's surgery, passing groups of excited and angry citizens on the way. Amelia Carstairs was in the surgery, still looking down at the body of her husband on the table they had placed him on, the doctor having finished his examination and standing by her comfortingly.

The wife of the banker was a handsome, upright woman, face drawn and pale but dry-eyed. I guess, thought Hezekiah, she will cry later in the privacy of her home and they will be genuine tears of regret and loss. She is a noble lady.

Amelia Carstairs turned her head to him as he came in. She said quietly, "When you catch up with them, Hezekiah, no shooting to kill unless you positively have to. I want to see them brought back and put on trial for this. We've had enough rough justice in this land. Let the law take its proper course."

Hezekiah touched his hat. "I will do what I can to bring that about, Amelia. But Jason was awful well liked. I don't guarantee to control all the itchy trigger fingers." He turned to go. "But I tell you this. We'll track 'em down if it takes from now until the day the Lord brings all sinners before the judgment bar."

Merrill, confident he had thrown off the raiders, rode on. It was dawn now and he had taken the chance to snatch a couple of hours' sleep.

In the light it was easier to pick one's way along the rock-bound trail with the jagged pinons often standing up as tall as a man, almost lined up like grim soldiers doing their best to keep out invaders.

It was getting towards the end of the day when suddenly Merrill's mount began to limp. He decided to make camp there and then. Maybe after a few hours' rest the lameness would go. After downing the coffee and cold beans he rolled himself up in his blanket.

But in the early dawn the horse was just as lame. Merrill cursed his luck again. He took a look around. Somehow he had a vaguely uneasy feeling that there were other riders in the vicinity.

139

He swung down off the lame horse and climbed up the side of the cliff face to get a better view. It was a peculiar place, different to all the other craggy heights he had passed.

It was pitted with caves and it had the overall look of a skull with the bony forehead on top, eyes in the form of two great caves placed in line with each other, a gaping slash in the cliff face that suggested a mouth and a gathering of rock beneath it that resembled a jaw. If he ever had to, he thought, he would know this place again without a doubt.

He kept going and stood up, looking back, the telescope in his hand he had taken out of a saddlebag. As he stared even without the aid of the telescope he could pick up tiny figures some miles in his rear. He put the telescope to his eye and picked them up clearly. After a minute or two he took the instrument away from his eye, cursing luridly.

It hadn't taken that one-eyed, one-handed sheriff any time at all to get hot on his trail with a posse. With a lame horse it was only a matter of time until they caught him. Merrill stood thinking. Then suddenly he made up his mind and scrambled back down to the waiting horse.

Quickly he pulled the small canvas sacks out of the saddlebags and, lumping them in his arms, he climbed slowly back up the cliff face again. He entered one of the caves that resembled an eye in the skull face of the cliff and went down its full length. Down at the far end he found a heap of rubble that had fallen down from the wall of the cave at some time.

He dug deep into the pile, scooping out great handfuls. Then he placed the sacks in the hole and went back for the others. When he had buried them all under the rubble he went back to the horse, taking a final look at the cliff face in the shape of a human skull. He had it imprinted on his mind as if he had taken a photograph of it.

He mounted the horse and rode on

slowly, the animal still limping. He knew that the posse was bound to catch him up, the sheriff knowing these canyons so well, but he banked on Hezekiah not being the lynching type.

When the posse came in sight Merrill put up his hands. Hezekiah rode up. He said abruptly, "Found your three friends back there. Looks like Big Knife Benito been at work on one big fat brother. Other two with bullet holes in 'em. The Mex raiders, huh?"

Merrill nodded. "Couldn't hold 'em off. We all made a break for it but I'm the only one that got away."

Hezekiah said curtly, "Didn't look to me like the other three was makin' a break for it when they got chopped down. Seem to me like you run out on 'em."

Merrill shrugged. The posse had circled him now, fixing the gambler with ugly looks, one man tentatively fingering the rope on his saddle horn.

Hezekiah shot a warning look at the rider. "You got better uses for your rope than this hombre's miserable neck, Cy. We're takin' him in to stand trial. Anyone thinks otherwise got me to deal with."

There were some discomfited rumblings but nobody fancied crossing their iron-hard sheriff. Hezekiah fixed his eye sternly on the gambler. "Folks said you rode off with a pack-mule. What happened to it?"

Merrill said coolly, "The raiders picked it up, with the other horses. And everything in its saddlebags."

Hezekiah said evenly, "You tellin' me them Mex raiders got everything you stole from the bank?"

Merrill said flatly, "That's about the size of it, sheriff."

Hezekiah stared at him in silence. Finally he said slowly, "Well, easy seen you ain't got it now. You ain't buried it somewhere — on the trail by any chance?"

Merrill threw his hand in a circle. "In this wilderness where everything looks the same? How would I ever find it again, sheriff? Look, when those raiders caught us up and outnumbered us three to one there was only one thought left to any of us — staying alive. When your life is in the balance, sheriff, you are not interested in hanging on to gold."

Hezekiah narrowed his eye a little more into a speculative squint. "An' you made sure that yours was gunna be one life that the raiders didn't take? But maybe you'd done better to stay and die with your friends. 'Cos looks like one way or another you're gunna end up hangin' or spending the rest of your life behind bars."

★ ★ ★

John Slade was seated in Rachel Jones' sitting room, eyes fixed on the schoolteacher.

Rachel sat facing him, hands folded, a slight flush on her cheeks. She said almost inaudibly and with a touch of awkwardness, "I am so pleased you called, John. It seems that I have scarcely conducted myself as a so-called educated woman in all of this." A wry smile flickered at one corner of her mouth. "I had thought I was something of a judge of character. Evidently in that area I am more of a fool."

Slade spread out his big rough hands, moved by her self-castigation. "Rachel, Merrill is a man with a tongue smooth as butter and a style to match. Combined with that he is a right smart dresser and got all the gallant ways of one of them southern planters. It ain't any wonder he got you all fired up — "

The girl smiled a little shamefacedly and the schoolteacher in her couldn't help saying, "It isn't any wonder, John." A little frown creased her forehead. "But I wonder about that. Why should it be no wonder that he could so — so intrigue me and yet I couldn't see what he really was?"

Slade said patiently, "Happens like those kind of men are expert at seeming to be someone else. It's like they put on a mask. Didn't they do that in them old Greek plays long back? Ole teacher in my schooldays tole me about it once. Didn't get much schoolin' but I always remember what he tole us that day. Sorta stuck in the mind. He said those oletime actors way long ago used to put on a mask when they wanted to look mean, another one when they wanted to 'pear kind and good, another one for somethin' else. Myron Merrill's that kind of man."

Rachel looked at him as if seeing him clearly for the first time. "You said that well, John. If you had been in one of my classes I would have given you top marks for knowing that about ancient Greek drama."

John Slade shook his head. "Ain't much I know about things like that but I do know I would never start pretendin' I was somethin' else other than what I am."

Rachel stared at him appraisingly. "No, I am sure you wouldn't, John.

146

You are a very honest man." She got to her feet. "I'll make us some coffee while you stay and we talk a little more."

As she left to go to the kitchen John Slade's eyes followed her admiringly. Things were getting to where they used to be before Myron Merrill's cavalier-like presence had appeared on the stage. Slade felt a new confidence about himself and this girl whom he knew no other could displace in his life.

When he finally left to go and Rachel had said her goodnight at the door he climbed on his horse and rode down into the town. He stopped at the home of the Carstairs, dismounted and went up to the front door. Sheree opened it, staring in surprise at him. "Why, John, what — "

Slade said shortly, "Sheree, I called to personally express my sympathy to Miz Carstairs and also to speak a word with you, if that's okay."

Sheree looked at him more closely,

a question in her eyes. "Yes, John, of course. Come through and see Amelia." The banker's widow rose as they came into the sitting room. "Why, John Slade, this is nice."

The farmer inclined his head. He said with his usual directness, "Jest came, Miz Carstairs, to say how I feel about your losing Jason. Your man was as straight as a gun barrel and the sort of citizen every town needs to build on for the future. Glad to know them varmints got caught up with one way and another. If I had been in town when that posse was called together I'd have been first man to join it. But failin' that all I can say is your Jason was a loss to us all."

Amelia Carstairs nodded and smiled. "Thank you, John." She nodded at the girl. "Sheree has been a great help — almost like having my own daughter. Let me tell you, John, anyone who gets her is going to be a very lucky man."

Slade winced. He cleared his throat. "I guess you're right, ma'am. As a

148

matter of fact, I meant to have a word with Sheree, too."

Amelia Carstairs smiled at them both. "Well, I'll just leave you two to have your chat." She nodded at Sheree. "I guess you and John have a few things to say to each other."

When she had gone, Sheree looked at him directly. "What is it, John?"

Slade cleared his throat again. This, he knew, would not be easy. "Sheree, now that Merrill's been brought back by Hezekiah things have changed a little."

The girl's eyes searched his unswervingly. "In what way, John?"

Slade raised his big hands a little helplessly. He said haltingly, "Well, I figure that Rachel's eyes have been opened. I've just been to see her — "

Sheree raised her voice a little. "Oh, yes?"

Slade faltered a little more. "Well, you see, I guess she was just fooled a little by him — "

The girl raised her eyebrows sarcastically. "A real bright schoolmarm fooled by that faker?"

Slade blundered on, "I guess she ain't been around like you have, Sheree."

She said fiercely, "What's that supposed to mean? That I've just been a saloon floozie and she's been a prim and proper lady?"

John Slade winced. "Sheree, you are a fine girl. But I guess there's only one I ever really wanted to make my wife an' it's still Rachel." He dropped his hands helplessly. "You see, Sheree, I just, well, I just plain love her."

Sheree's face, hardened by what he had had to say, softened a little. She said briskly, "Well, you've said what you came to say, John. It wasn't exactly what I was dying to hear but it's been said." She went to the front door and opened it. "You'd better go, John."

* * *

In her sitting room Emily Anderson said slowly to Hezekiah, "You know, what Merrill has done has changed a lot of things. It's made Amelia a widow, Rachel Jones has been sadly disillusioned and John Slade who was sort of taking up with that girl Sheree is bound to leave her and go back to Rachel."

Hezekiah squinted at her. "Why is John gunna do that?"

Emily said, raising her eyebrows, "Because he really loves Rachel, that's why."

10

A Knife for Apache Joe

IN the wickiup Juanita was working on the jacket. Apache Joe looked lovingly at his favourite squaw. "That is a beautiful jacket you are making for me."

The girl looked back at him, eyes flashing. "It will far outshine the gringo cavalryman's coat that Blue Jacket wears, my husband."

Apache Joe frowned a little. "He speaks nothing but war to our young bronco bucks."

The chief got up from the cougar skin where he had been squatting cross-legged and moved across to the girl. He gently rested a hand on her gleaming braided hair that was as black as an Indian's.

A figure moved through the entrance

of the pole and brush hut. Apache Joe turned to look. It was Blue Jacket. He said surlily, "I come to talk."

Apache Joe faced him angrily. "Your talk is always of war. You would bring the world down upon us until we are destroyed. There is time for other things than war — "

Blue Jacket thundered, "Dead chiefs don't give orders!" His knife flashed in the air, glittering death. Apache Joe staggered back, mouth open with shock, a great bloody gash where the weapon had torn into his chest. Blood rushed out of his mouth and he fell, his eyes closing.

Blue Jacket glared at the prostrate chief and without a word stalked out of the wickiup.

The girl, struck dumb with fear and shock, rushed across to Apache Joe. What she did then was purely by instinct. She put her hands under the arms of the apparently lifeless chief, blood still pouring from his wound, and dragged him to the entrance of the hut. She ran into another squaw about to enter, mouth hanging loose as she also took in the scene.

Juanita gabbled something at the newcomer and ran. The squaw stayed by the chief, making quick use of her clothing to help staunch the blood. Shortly the girl returned. She was leading two horses, a roan mustang mare and a dun pony. Between them, she and the other squaw got the body of the chief across the back of the roan mare, the horse rearing a little at the smell of blood.

Juanita leapt on the back of the dun-coloured pony and trotted off leading the mare carrying the body of the chief. The path she took was wild and rocky, apparently leading nowhere. After a few miles her destination came in sight. It was a broken-down ranch-house, obviously abandoned by its original owner.

A tall man with shoulder-length white hair and wearing a high-crowned black hat came out to the front of the house, calling the dogs back. Juanita slid down off her mount. She called, "Jacobo, great chief, help me — "

The tall man, old as he was, even ancient, had a long, free stride. As he joined the girl she said, breathing hard, "It is the work of Blue Jacket. He wants to be numero uno — "

The tall man grunted. He swung the body of Apache Joe over his shoulders and carried him to the ranch house as if he was a child. Inside he laid the chief gently on a ramshackle bed and began stripping off his clothes to get at the wound. He and the girl worked quickly to clean and bandage the great gash, not speaking in their concentration. The tall man with hands gentle as a woman laid the white-faced, unconscious chief back on the bed and they left the room quietly.

The girl said tensely, "I brought him to you because if Blue Jacket thought he was not dead he would have come back and — finito. And then you are the great chief who left the tribe finally after many years of leadership to come and commune here alone with the spirits. I knew he would be safe here. First, because you are the great one whom my people the Mexicans called Jacobo and lived in fear of your name and also because you talk with the spirits and the bronco braves are afraid that if they cross you in any way you may cast a death spell on them."

The old chief looked sombre. He said, his voice deep and dignified, "He will take time to heal. But I can speed that with herbs I know of. Let the tribe know that if any come to harm him while he is laid low the curse of Usen will fall upon them."

Juanita shivered a little at the name of the almighty Apache God. She moved to the door.

★ ★ ★

In Davenport Tommy Turner was hustling before him a little thin, narrow-shouldered man wearing sandals, loose-fitting shirt and trousers and with a blanket slung over one shoulder Mexican style.

Reaching the sheriff's office, Tommy snapped at the man he was escorting, "Inside, Miguel. Let's see what the sheriff thinks of you." The thin little man shrugged his shoulders and shuffled through the open door.

Hezekiah looked up from his desk. The deputy nodded at the man he had brought in. "This here hombre says his name is Miguel Montez." He frowned a little. "How come so many of these greasers got that moniker Miguel?"

"Spanish of Michael," said Hezekiah. "Guess we got a few Michaels, too."

Tommy went on, giving the Mexican a suspicious look. "Says he's one of them peons. Romero raided a village and took a few people, men and women, to work for him. This little greaser says he never worked so hard in his life. Only got the leavin's of the food. Anytime he didn't do anything right got whipped with a quirt."

Hezekiah eyed the little Mexican appraisingly. He rattled off a torrent in Spanish at him. The man's eyes brightened as he joined in rapid fire conversation with the sheriff. Finally Hezekiah abruptly cut off the talk.

He turned his gaze back on the deputy, Tommy looking piqued at not being able to follow the conversation with his sparse knowledge of Spanish. Hezekiah smiled his rare smile. "This here maid of all work been havin' a hard time. Far as I can see, Tommy, what he told you seems to square up with what I asked him. Tell you something. Get him a bed for the night some place and I'll talk with him again in the morning. This little greaser should be able to tell us a few interesting things about Romero and his doin's."

Tommy Turner grunted. He nodded

at the skinny little Mexican to follow him and the other man fell in behind him like a docile dog, flashing a grateful look at the sheriff as he went.

That night Hezekiah with his usual custom was reading from the big blackbound book. Merrill's voice came from his cell. "Would you put out that light, sheriff? I'd like to get some sleep."

Hezekiah glanced back at the cell. "Readin' from the Good Book, Merrill. Somethin' you shoulda done. Kept you out of where you are right now." Then he heard the creaking step on the boardwalk outside.

He stood up and moved fast away from the window where his upper body was throwing a shadow against the shade. The creaking sound had stopped instantly. Hezekiah spoke again in a normal tone but listening with the ear of an animal aware it is being hunted. He said loudly, "Yeah, that's what you should have done, Merrill.

Shoulda read what it says in that book of *Proverbs*. Says that in the long run there ain't no reward for the man who plans to rob and kill others. It says the expectation of the wicked shall perish."

Merrill's voice called, "Spare me the holy rhetoric, sheriff. I heard a preacher talking like that once. He had on a suit with patches in the pants. I was wearing something made by the best tailor in St Louis. I thought to myself, well, if that's how much your God allows you for clothes He hasn't got an awful lot of dress sense."

Hezekiah said loudly, "The best-dressed people often end up in the worst place; like hell, for instance."

He raised his voice, speaking very slowly and emphasising each word. "I am going to take a look outside to make sure all is quiet in the town. Then I'm gunna close up for the night, Merrill, and you can get your shut-eye." He said, raising his voice a little more, "I'll just take a peek out the door and then we can rest easy."

Merrill's voice started to say, "I'd be obliged if you'd just do it, sheriff, and not give me the details. I am just wanting — "

Hezekiah had reached the door and turned the knob. As he did so he threw himself to one side.

The Colt thundered from outside and Hezekiah almost felt the wind as the slug passed him. Gun already in his left hand, he fired three shots so fast they almost ran into one sound.

The figure standing outside swayed as if hit by a big wind and then fell in a heap on the boardwalk. Hezekiah moved across and looked down.

It was Miguel, the gunman posing as a refugee from Romero's camp. He was as dead as an ancient Aztec.

Merrill's voice rang out, "What in hell was all that?" Hezekiah called, "A message from Luis Romero that never got delivered."

As he went to pick up the dead

Mexican, he was thinking, Romero must think I am important to the defence of this town. One thing for sure — looks like he is really headed this way.

11

Sheree Takes a Hand

SHEREE BRODIE looked across the supper table at Amelia Carstairs, gauging what would be the older woman's response before she spoke. The girl said abruptly, "I've been thinking about paying a visit to Myron Merrill." Amelia gave her a surprised look. "What on earth for, my dear?"

Sheree said slowly, "We had a relationship once. He wasn't always what he turned out to be here in Davenport. There were times when he — well, we got along pretty well. I'd like to see if there's anything left in him of those days. At times he was decent and honest. It would be a good thing at the trial if he decided to be open about it all — to tell how it all happened without lying and trying to cover up."

Amelia looked at her keenly. "You know, of course, if he did that he could possibly lose a chance of receiving a lighter sentence. It would all depend how the judge looked at it."

The girl nodded. "I understand that. But, just for old times sake, I would like to see him end up like a man — not like some cheap hold-up thief who added murder to his crime."

Amelia said slowly, "Well, of course, the tellers both told us that it was the other man, that ex-cowboy, who shot and killed Jason."

Sheree nodded again. "Yes, but Myron might as well have pulled the trigger. I'd like to see if he has any remorse.

"I doubt it, my dear. But if he has any feelings of regret for what he has done it would be something in his favour." She smiled at the girl. "If you feel this way I suppose a visit from you would not be out of the way."

Sheree said decisively, "I'll call on

him tonight." After the meal she put on a shoulder cape and bonnet and went out, heading for the jailhouse.

At her knock she heard the little dog bark as Hezekiah came to the door. His one eye stared surprisedly at her. Sheree asked, "Can I see your prisoner?" Hezekiah kept staring. "Well, I guess so." He looked down at the handbag she carried. "You ain't got a file in that, have you?"

Sheree shook her head, smiling faintly. "No. Myron and I had an association before we both came to Davenport, as I told you before. I just want to talk to him about what he's done and maybe encourage him to be as honest as possible at the trial."

Hezekiah touched the hook to his chin to scratch it gently. "Well, now, that trial don't look like comin' off for a while. Judges, it seems, are pretty busy people and also travelling down in these parts ain't the most healthy thing to be doing right now."

He said soberly, "But if you can get

Merrill to open up at the trial it would sure help proceedings and might even give him a better chance of cheating the hangman."

He took her down to the cell door, the little dog with them growling through the bars at the prisoner, and left her there. Merrill, sitting on the edge of his bunk, stared unbelievingly at the girl. "Sheree — I never thought — "

He came across to the bars and already he was adopting his customary polished manner. "Well, you are certainly an improvement on the faces of that one-eyed sheriff and his sawn-off deputy. What brings you here? Dare I ask, for old times' sake?"

The girl took hold of the bars in her two gloved hands. "All my memories of that are not bad, Myron. You had a way of spending money on a woman and also of courting her in a way that was not unattractive."

The gambler grinned. "Most of my ladies thought it was damn attractive. Especially that Creole. That's what really turned you against me, wasn't it? My taking up with her."

Sheree said with a flash of anger, "Dropping me like you did and paying court to that half-breed, beautiful as she was, would have got you a knife in the back from a lot of women."

Merrill touched one of her hands on the bars. He said urgently, "She was the most expensive disaster I ever got caught up with. Less than a month after I picked her up she took off with a planter who had more money than Midas, the king whose touch turned everything to gold." He grinned. "Only no one's touch could do that with that coloured woman. She was genuine lead from top to bottom. You were the gold I threw away, Sheree."

The girl said cuttingly, "Then why did you pick up with that schoolteacher, that Rachel Jones?"

Merrill gave his easy, half-mocking smile. "She is a very good-looking woman and I am a man who must have some feminine interest in his life.

Besides, it gave me a chance to show her the difference between that farmer she had calling on her and a man who knew his way around the world."

Sheree said with a touch of malice, "She's gone back to that farmer now and her view of you is considerably less than it was." Merrill shrugged. He shot a satirical glance at her. "And doesn't that also mean that the farmer had left you to take up with her again?"

Sheree said shortly, "We all make our mistakes." She dropped her hands from the bars and stepped back a little. She eyed him sharply. "When the trial comes how you going to handle your side of it?"

Merrill lowered his voice. "As defensively as I can. I am going to do everything to get the lightest sentence possible. One reason is that I can point out that Hank Smith and not me shot Jason Carstairs." He paused a moment. "And I have another very special reason."

Hezekiah came limping towards them.

"I figure you two have done enough talkin' over old times." He nodded at the girl. "If you want to see the prisoner again, come another time. This man looks like having folks come to call on him in jail for a long time."

Sheree stepped aside. She looked strangely at Merrill. She said quickly, "Maybe you'll tell me what that other special reason is next time I come."

Hezekiah said, "Next time maybe my deputy will be on duty. Don't mind his scattergun. He'll only use it if Merrill tries to break loose. In that case, Tommy will make it hard for you to talk to more than one piece of the prisoner at a time."

When Sheree walked back to the Carstairs home she was thinking, maybe next time Merrill would tell her that second special reason he had for trying to get a light sentence.

When Sheree called to visit Merrill again Tommy Turner let her in. He said to her in his blunt little deputy manner, "Shoulda thought a good-lookin' gal like you woulda had better ways to fill in her evenin's than callin' on a bank-robber."

Sheree muttered something about having known Merrill a long time as Tommy led her to the cell. The little deputy snorted, "Shoulda taught you that once a coyote always a coyote." He went back to his chair in the office.

Merrill came over to the cell door, all smiling welcome. Sheree said immediately, "You told me you had two reasons for wanting to get a light sentence and the second one was very special. What is it?"

Merrill surveyed her carefully. He said slowly, "What would you say to taking a long trip with me — around the world maybe in the best of style?"

She gave him a withering look. "You crazy? Here you are locked up and maybe facing even a life sentence and you talk like that!"

Merrill insisted, "If what I said was possible, would you come with me?

You always said you wanted to see places like Venice and Rome, London and Paris."

Sheree stared. "What are you talking about?"

Merrill shot a glance through the bars at Tommy Turner. The deputy was far enough away not to hear them clearly but near enough to see their every move. The little deputy evidently was more concerned with what may have looked like unlawful action than he was with conversation.

Merrill lowered his voice. He reached through the bars and touched Sheree's arm. "Listen, kid, what's for you in a town like this? Nothing. That farmer guy you thought was sweet on you has gone back to his schoolmarm lady love. All you'll end up doing here is working in that dry goods store the rest of your life. If you listen to me and show a little sense I can promise you to see the Taj Mahal, the fountains of Rome, Buckingham Palace, the islands of the South Seas — "

Sheree broke in. "And how long do I have to wait before you can give me all this?"

Merrill's face took on a sharp, tense edge. "If you're smart, not very long at all."

"And where," asked the girl mockingly, "is all the money coming from?"

Merrill lowered his voice a little. "You'd be surprised how much money was in that bank." Sheree stared at him silently for a moment. "You mean — "

Merrill hissed, "Help me get out of here and we split it fifty-fifty."

The little deputy stared across at them. "Cut out that whisperin', you two. Don't sound right." Merrill raised his voice. "Okay, deputy. But sometimes it's nice to talk about things that are private matters."

"Ain't nothin' private in the hoose-gow," grumbled Tommy. Merrill agreed. "You're so right, deputy." He lowered his voice again just a fraction, speaking out of the corner of his mouth.

"I've let you in on something, Sheree,

because I've taken a chance on you. You've got two choices. One is, tell what I've told you to the sheriff. If you do, I'll deny it to his face. Say that you are a disappointed lover who is trying to get back at me. The other choice is, help me get out of here and your dreams about seeing the world can be as real and beautiful as sunrise in Hawaii."

The girl stood staring at him, turning it all over in her mind.

Tommy Turner stumped towards them, voice gruff and impatient. "This ain't a public meetin' place. You better git movin', girlie. We got sorta visitin' hours here and your time is up."

Back in her room at Amelia Carstairs' home that night Sheree had a dream. It was of sands crashing on white beaches, the velvet glamour of nights in Spain, the glittering slopes of snow-clad Alps, the bridges of Paris . . . The dream woke her up and had her staring into the night, wondering.

★ ★ ★

A couple of evenings later Hezekiah lifted a table napkin to his mouth and dabbed it there with satisfaction. "Emily, if you were to take a notion to runnin' a hotel in this town and kept on serving up grub like that you would be a rich woman in no time at all."

Emily Anderson said flatly, "Feeding you and occasionally that hungry deputy of yours is enough time in the kitchen for me. I would sooner keep on selling canned food across the counter of my store." She asked soberly, "Hezekiah, what do you make of Sheree calling on Myron Merrill so often?"

The sheriff looked thoughtful. "I figure they must have been pretty close in the past. People that live the way they have are nacherally drawn to each other. That gal has talked about Merrill being all sorts of a double-crossing man earlier in her life but when the chips are down people who have lived around saloons always seem to wind up in each other's company."

Emily demurred, "But Sheree strikes me as being an honest girl."

Hezekiah shrugged. "Maybe so. But she and Merrill would have as much in common their way as you and me have in our way."

"Do you think she is really sympathetic to him? I can hardly believe that, because in the short time she was with them before Jason got killed she was very close with the Carstairs."

The sheriff nodded. "Yeah. Well, changed she might have been but you can't wipe out in a short time what you might have shared together over a long time." He grinned. "Also maybe she's taking the chance while he's cooped up there to tell him clear and plain what she thinks of him for having run out on her before they both finished up here. John Slade said that girl told him about that one night."

Emily shook her head. "I'm glad nothing really came of her and Slade.

I feel, as I said, that Sheree is a good honest girl but Rachel has always been the one for John." The sheriff kept grinning. "Like they say about you and me."

Emily said grimly, "I've given you my answer to that, Hezekiah. If you ever want my hand you'd better pass in your badge first." A little frown creased her forehead. "But I certainly hope for Sheree's sake she is not falling under that suave man's spell again."

Hezekiah said comfortably, "Well, he's fixed so he can't do her any harm and after the judge comes he'll be able to do her even less."

Emily said quietly, "I hope you're right. But I just feel a little uneasy about it . . . "

* * *

Sheree pulled the horses up behind the jailhouse. She got off her mount and let the reins of the other saddlehorse and the packhorse trail. She walked around to the front of the jailhouse and knocked.

Tommy Turner shambled to the door, mumbling something about dang-busted callers in the night. He opened the door growling, "Now, listen here, young lady — " but stopped short as he found himself staring down the barrel of the Colt Sheree held firmly on him. She said tersely, "Move back in, deputy, and don't make a sound."

Tommy, staring unbelievingly, backed into the office. Sheree moved in, quickly, shutting the door behind her. She snapped, "Get the keys. We're letting your prisoner loose."

Tommy was still struggling with what was happening. He moved as if in a dream back to where he had been sitting and took the keys to the cell door from the big hook they hung on. Still unable to find words and staring as if hypnotised at the gun held on him by the girl he went across and unlocked the cell for a grinning Merrill to step out.

The gambler said exultantly, "That's

my girl. That's the Sheree I used to know." He had brought a blanket out with him and already he was tearing it into strips. Sheree gestured with the gun for Tommy to go into the cell. The deputy, found voice. "Why, you skulkin', double-crossin pair — " His hand crept towards the gun holstered at his hip but Merrill slapped his hand down and unbuckled the gun belt around the deputy's waist to strap it around his own.

Merrill pushed the deputy back on to the bunk and in a moment or two had tied his hands behind his back and his ankles together. Before the deputy could say another word the gambler had tied a gag tightly about his mouth as he lay on the bunk.

Sheree and Merrill stepped out through the cell door, locking it behind them and throwing the keys on the floor. Merrill stayed to take a rifle out of a rack of weapons in the sheriff's office and to find and pocket a couple of boxes of shells.

Moving fast, the two went out the back door of the jail to the horses waiting outside. They mounted swiftly and went off at a swift trot, Merrill leading the packhorse behind. A hoot-owl cried out somewhere but otherwise all was quiet.

Merrill followed the same trail he had taken on a former occasion with the two deaf mutes and Hank Smith. They covered the early ground at speed, driving the horses on, putting as much ground between them and the inevitable pursuing posse while the going was good. With luck, Merrill thought, back in Davenport they wouldn't find out about the break for hours. He and the girl would have put a lot of miles behind them by then. He looked across at Sheree riding beside him and thought, why I ever took up with that Creole when I had this girl beside me I'll never know.

Sheree was silent, staring determinedly ahead as she rode. Merrill thought, she's thinking of the money and those places of glamour and beauty she's going to see. He exulted, and I'll show her every last one of them.

An hour or so later they ran into the Badlands and they slowed down. Later still, before dawn, Merrill signalled to Sheree to pull up. As they got down off their mounts he said briefly, "We'll rest up a while. Don't want to kill the horses. Then we'll push on."

The girl, still silent, nodded. Merrill thought, that's what I like. A woman who does things instead of talking.

When the light came they went on, making the best time they could over the brutal ground.

Hours later they made another halt. Merrill was scanning the ground keenly. It was almost the identical trail he and the others had followed on their earlier ride. Hot mug of coffee in hand, he grinned across at Sheree. "We're making good time. Just hope we don't run into raiders. But luck's been with us so far. I feel we're on a winning streak."

The girl, sipping her coffee, regarded him steadily. "Money means a lot to you, doesn't it, Myron?" He asked, "Doesn't it to you?" The girl looked off into the distance, conjuring up other thoughts. "Well, when it's a means of seeing those places I've alreays dreamed of going to I guess it does."

"Right, kid, and you're going to see them all." He got to his feet, tossing away the dregs of his coffee and stamping out their small fire. He said briskly, "Let's hit this horror trail again. Guess it's just as much unholy travelling to whoever is following us and maybe getting further behind."

When they finally came to the place, Merrill's eyes glittered with expectancy. It was the skull's head that he had implanted deep in his mind.

His gaze went directly to the hole in the cliff that formed one of the eyes, the one in which he had dug down and secreted the loot. As he got off his horse he signalled to Sheree to also dismount. He said briefly, "We'll take the packhorse as far as he can climb. Then we'll go ahead on foot."

When they had got down to the farthermost recess of the cave Merrill got to his knees and began scratching furiously, shovelling up the dirt like a gopher burrowing out a subterannean runway.

When the first little canvas sack appeared he let out a whoop and held it aloft. "And there's more — " He started digging again, eyes only for the loot.

He hardly noticed Sheree drop down beside him. But when she pulled the gun out of the holster at his hip he swung his head around, startled. "Hey, what — "

The gun roared twice in the cave, the sound like thunder in the narrow confines. Merrill fell back, his face a bloody, blasted ruin. His body twitched once and the canvas sack fell out of his hand.

Sheree looked down at him. She said quietly, "Jason Carstairs was the sort of man you could never be."

She turned to scratching out the rest of the bags. When she had them all out she started taking them down to the packhorse.

* * *

Hezekiah saw the rider coming towards them, leading the other two horses and he put up the hook to halt the posse. When Sheree reached them she looked steadily at the sheriff. She said, "Everything Merrill and the others took from the bank is on that packhorse. If you want Myron Merrill he's back there in the cave where he buried it all last time. But he won't be able to tell you anything."

12

Blue Jacket Rides Out

THERE was turmoil and action in the rancheria as there had been since Apache Joe had gone and Blue Jacket had taken over the leadership. Put aside were the tasks of tanning hides, even hunting. The air was all for war.

Blue Jacket yelled, "This day we will ride and kill. There is cattle to be taken, horses to be driven off, ranch houses to be destroyed, men and women to die — " He lifted his voice higher. "Their young ones must die also. When the White-Eyes cavalry have raided our camps they have slain our children. They have said, 'Kill the nits for they will grow up to breed further lice.' Let us turn this back upon their own heads." He raised his voice even higher. "Enju! I have spoken!"

The roar came again, "Shis-Inday!" Blue Jacket wheeled his pony again and set his heels to its sides. The yelling company of bronco braves took off after him in a thundering cloud of dust and hoofbeats.

The old shaman, the medicine man, shambled out of his wickiup and stared after them through bleary eyes, shaking his head, Juanita, passing by, stopped at his side. She said anxiously, "Old man, can't you stop this madness?"

The shaman again sourly shook his head. "Blue Jacket has found a potion that is stronger than mine. It is a thing of blood and war. It rouses them to a great fury."

His eyes took on a look of apprehension. "But it can only mean one thing. The Nakai-Ye and the White-Eyes are like the locusts that come sometimes and devour everything. There is no end to them. We are but a small people. If we provoke these our enemies too greatly it will end in our destruction." He shot an appealing look at her. "You go to see your husband again soon? Tell him to get well and come back before Blue Jacket brings death upon us all." He shambled back into the wickiup.

Juanita's eyes flashed with sudden fire. Yes, Apache Joe was responding more every day to Jacobo's special ministrations. She would ride over that very day and see him. She looked around the rancheria with anxious eyes. Apache Joe would want to see it kept alive, not brought to know death and ruin.

★ ★ ★

That night in Davenport Emily Anderson welcomed Hezekiah as he stepped through her front door, little dog at his heels. Hezekiah looked at her questioningly. "Why did you ask me to specially bring Little Mister Short-tail along with me tonight?"

Emily bent down to pat the tiny dog

186

who licked her hand with affection as an old friend. She straightened up. "You'll see. I also did not ask you to bring Tommy with you because I have invited two other guests."

Hezekiah sat down, the little dog curling up at his feet. "And who might they be?"

Emily looked at him solemnly. "Rachel Jones and Sheree Brodie." Hezekiah stared, surprised. "Hey, is that wise? Ain't John Slade been courtin' 'em both? Far as I know, that always tends to spark a certain amount of enmity between young ladies." He looked reminiscent. "Y'know, in the Good Book it says King David had seventeen wives. That's as I counted 'em, anyways. An' I often thought to myself, seventeen women scrappin' over one man. How'd he ever keep 'em in order?"

Emily said firmly, "I don't think there'll be any scrapping here tonight with these two." She looked at him appealingly. "Hezekiah, I've brought them together because I think they are two fine girls who need to be friends. Now, I want you to help me bring that about." She added, "Incidentally, neither of them knows I asked the other one here tonight."

Hezekiah cleared his throat. "Seems like my helpin' out will have to be pretty fancy." He looked down at the little dog. "An' how does Mister Short-tail figure in all this?" Emily nodded confidently. "You'll see."

There was a knock at the door. She said briskly, "There's the first of the girls now." She came back with Rachel Jones. The schoolteacher looked surprisedly at the sheriff, nodding greetings. Then her eyes wandered to the little dog who had come to his feet at her arrival. A look of pleasure came across Rachel's face.

"What a dear little fellow — " She bent straight down to fondle the little creature, all smiles. Mister Short-tail responded to her happily. Hezekiah said, "That's a big plus for you, missy.

That little critter can smell out the good from the bad quicker than a thirsty cow can smell water in a dry land."

The girl, smiling, put the little dog down, still patting him. Emily excused herself, going out to the kitchen to put the finishing touches to the meal. When she came back there was another knock at the door. Emily went off and came back with Sheree Brodie.

When the two girls' eyes met they stiffened. Sheree said coldly, "Oh, I didn't know — if I had I wouldn't have — " The little dog came across to her, sniffing her shoe. Sheree looked down and immediately her face softened. She bent down and scooped the little dog up in her arms. He let her lift him unprotesting licking her face as she drew him up closer.

Hezekiah stared. "Last time I saw someone do that to him apart from here tonight he bit their finger nigh to the bone. He is really a sorta one-man dog but he seems to have found a coupla new friends right here." Emily bustled around. "I've set a place for Mister Short-tail in the kitchen and after he's eaten he can come back and join us."

It was after the meal and everything cleared away that Emily looked directly at the two girls. "I asked you both here tonight because I want to see you become friends."

Both girls opened their mouths to say something but Emily held up her hand to silence them. She went on quickly, "You are both fine young women. I don't care what Sheree may have done before but what she did about Jason and the stolen money was something only a woman with real spunk and a capacity for loyalty to a fine man and his wife could have done. And you, Rachel, you are a boon to the children of this town and our hope is that you will marry a certain young farmer and settle down here for good."

She looked back at the other girl. "And there's plenty of other young men who would line up to make you the same offer, Sheree." She finished with a burst. "And I'm sure that Little Mister Short-tail there backs up everything I've said." The little dog, as if in response to her words, got to his feet and gave two sharp, happy barks.

"That," said Hezekiah, "is prob'ly the veal you fed him talkin' but he sure said it at the right time."

The two girls, faces softening and as if acting on the one impulse, dropped to their knees to reach out towards the little dog. As their hands met they smiled at each other, Mister Short-tail wriggling good-temperedly in their grasp.

Later when he was leaving, following the two girls who had gone out together, Hezekiah stopped at the door. He said, "Y'know, Emily, you didn't invite me here tonight. You invited Mister Short-tail."

"And," said Emily, contented, "he did what my old aunt Sophia would have called a right smart job."

191

At Jacobo's ranch with the saguaro cactus standing up like prickly sentinels before the house Juanita got off her pony. As she went up to the house the old chief came to meet her. His usually sombre face was alive, smiling.

"Your man, your chief, he is finding health and strength again. I have not forgotten my arts since I came here. He will be well and strong and he will lead the tribe again."

Juanita's eyes darkened. "It will be difficult, old one. Blue Jacket has the warriors blood-crazy. They ride out every day to kill and plunder. They cut down everyone . . . Mexicans, whites, anyone they see as the enemy. To regain control of them again will be hard, very hard, for my husband to do."

Jacobo said bluntly, "He is a strong man, a lion. Blue Jacket is a mad coyote. A mountain lion can overcome a coyote any time."

Juanita murmured, "It was the coyote who brought down the lion last time." Jacobo frowned. "That was treachery. A chief does not expect naked treachery from one who should be his loyal follower." He brightened. "But come and see your husband. He grows stronger every day."

When he took her inside the girl saw Apache Joe walking about, a little stiff-gaited but obviously well on the mend. She ran to him with a small cry and he took her gently into his arms. He released her to look at her, smiling. "I have a fine healer, my wife. He gives me medicine that brings tears to my eyes and foulness to my mouth but it puts life into my bones again." He asked anxiously, "How goes the rancheria?"

Juanita grew tense. "Badly, my husband. Blue Jacket rides out day after day, leading the warriors. Always they come back with blood on their hands and a missing rider or two. But they keep following him. He has cast a spell over them, a dream of great victory, of driving out all the whites and the Mexicans simply by killing them all — "

Apache Joe said fiercely, "I must go back. Another few days and I will be even stronger. It will come to a duel. If I can win back the leadership in hand to hand combat I will lead them as they should be led."

★ ★ ★

Blue Jacket's band was advancing through the canyon towards the White-Eyes' farm they knew lay immediately beyond when the two scouts came galloping back.

One raced straight up to the chief, breathless. He gasped, "Back there — Romero's Raiders, coming towards us — a big force. They saw us and some are in pursuit — "

Blue Jacket's eyes flashed. "These are our great enemies — maybe even worse than the blancos. They want to take all our land. They say they have a great claim because their ancestors came here many moons ago." There was blazing hate in his eyes. "But our people were here before their ancestors, before time itself — "

He turned on the warriors behind him, waving his carbine in an almost insane spirit of defiance. "This is our chance to wipe out these Nakai-Ye, these invaders, led by this terrible grandee."

He lifted himself up on the back of his pony and screamed, "Curses and destruction on all Nakai-Ye!" The warriors galloped after him, whooping and yelling. It was when they rounded the next bend that they met the hail of bullets like a sudden blinding thunderstorm on the prairie.

Two braves dropped from their saddles, cut down by the withering blast. Blue Jacket led the return of fire but soon all the Indians were sliding off their ponies and scrambling for cover behind the rocks.

One of the scouts got alongside Blue Jacket. He shouted above the roar of gunfire, "They are not as many as I thought. We can match them — "

Blue Jacket smiled grimly. "We can do more — we can send them to the Big Sleep, every last cursed one of them!"

The raiders were also dismounting and were sheltering behind rocks as they kept up a steady fire. Blue Jacket caught a glimpse of Romero, a tall striking figure with a huge black sombrero decorated with silver pesos.

Blue Jacket fired a couple of shots at him but the raiders' leader, as always, seemed to bear a charmed life. The Indian cursed and directed his fire elsewhere.

One of the raiders, lacking caution, came into view around a boulder. A bronco buck, taking careful aim, shot him through the head and the man flopped back, dead. The Indians whooped with delight.

But suddenly they noticed something else.

Gunfire was coming at them from a different direction. Heads turned quickly and they could see more raiders coming down on them from the top of the canyon behind them. It dawned on Blue Jacket what had happened.

Romero, after sighting the Apaches, had sent some of his troops up along a trail on top of the canyon to get past the Indians and to come in on them from behind. That was why the scout had thought he had been mistaken about their number.

Blue Jacket gritted his teeth. They were caught between two fires now and had no chance of returning both effectively. He could see the only thing to do was to retreat. Even as the thought flashed through his mind it was reinforced by the sight of one of his braves, bullet-ridden, sliding down a boulder which had been his shelter until the attack came from behind.

Blue Jacket, raging inside, but with no choice, gave the signal to his braves to run for their horses and escape. Even as they ran two more braves fell, cut down by the raking double fire.

They scrambled on their ponies and, lying low on their necks, raced back towards the end of the canyon through which they had entered it.

As they rode, Blue Jacket suddenly felt a streak of fire drive into his back like a javelin hurled from the hand of a giant. That was the last thing he ever knew.

* * *

Two nights later Apache Joe limped into the rancheria to speak to a disheartened, diminished band of warriors, something less than those who had gone out a couple of days before whooping for blood. The shaman stood alongside him. The old man seemed to have grown in both physical and emotional stature.

The shaman bit out to the gathered warriors, "You chose to follow a madman. He led you into a trap that meant death for some of you — more than we can afford to lose. You turned your back on your lawful chief and followed one whose dreams were vain and unreal."

He stabbed a finger at Apache Joe. "This is your true chief. He comes back to you still a little weak from that treacherous attack but he is gathering strength day by day. He led you well in the past and he will lead you that way again. Follow him, even if it means joining up with the blancos of Davenport to help drive out those raiders who not only kill the old and the weak but rape our women. Listen to him! Enju!"

Apache Joe stood up before them, looking around. He could see rows of chastened faces expressing regret and a fresh obedience. Inwardly thanking Usen for a faithful wife and a healer like Jacobo, he began to speak.

13

A Call on Slade

THERE was great excitement in the town of San Cristobal, the largest in that area of the state of Sonora, just over the border from Arizona Territory. The great Luis Romero, leader of the famous Raiders and maybe a prime candidate for the presidency of the nation of Mexico, had come to speak to them.

The people, in tattered pants, worn sandals and thread-bare serapes, crowded in to the city hall, amongst them numbers of half-breeds, mestizos of mixed Spanish and Indian blood, the word meaning mongrel, also goatherds, simple farming peasants, people also of substance and wealth sitting up front separated from the hoi-polloi.

In the town's main building on

a platform at one end there sat the alcalde, the mayor, and other dignitaries. Luis Romero emerged on the stage, a magnificent figure in beautifully embroidered jacket, tight-fitting velvet trousers flared at the ends, frilled white shirt and silver ornamentation all over.

He was a stunningly impressive man with hair that shone like jet polished to a high gleam. A fine black moustache decked his upper lip and he had the hawk-like handsomeness of a conquistador.

But his eyes were the eyes of a renegade wolf. At his appearance there burst forth a storm of applause, led by his own Raiders and the menacing rurales.

Romero looked around him. He shouted, "Fellow countrymen, we have a great task before us. Our aim is to repossess, to take hold again of the land stolen from us by the Americans." Cheering, again led by the Raiders and the rurales, broke out.

Romero, eyes flashing, went on. "In 1848 in that treacherous agreement with the United States called the treaty of Hidalgo we lost nearly half the land that properly belonged to Mexico. And then again six years later our own government betrayed us further by selling more land to the United States to put their cursed railroad through. Yet in that land lies buried copper, silver and gold that is rightfully ours."

His voice rose higher. "We must take it back and in doing so also obliterate the Indian scum that still inhabits much of it." He raised a fist and shook it. "All true Mexicans must stand with me and help me build a force that will take me to the presidency and better times for all!"

By now even the docile members of the crowd had caught something of his fervour and were beginning to rise to their feet and shout with excitement. The Raiders and rurales were literally thundering their approval, wolves howling for blood, stirred up by a leader with a purpose that had become a mania with him which he was transmitting to them.

★ ★ ★

A few days after the meeting led by Romero in San Cristobal, Hezekiah and Tommy Turner were heading once more to the outlying farms and ranches of the county. With the custom of horsemen on a long ride they had not spoken much but suddenly Hezekiah broke the silence. "This maybe gotta be our last warning, deputy."

Tommy grunted agreement. "Yeah. If they don't wanta pack up and come into the town ain't much more we can do."

Hezekiah nodded towards the northeast. "John Slade is the furthest out. John is a mighty plucky man and a rare good shot but one man on his own ain't gunna hold off a pack of raiders with Benito dyin' to get his big knife at someone's throat. Let's ride out that way."

Tommy grunted again and turned his horse in the same direction. It was when they had drawn within sight of the farmhouse that they heard the shots.

Hezekiah muttered, "The Lord musta given me a nudge in this direction."

Tommy Turner shook his head. "You sure git them visions or whatever, Hezekiah." He dug his heels into his mount. "Let's git up thar an' see what's doin'."

Riding at a gallop they could see a few men in their familiar sombreros, white garments and bandoliers crossed over the shoulders in the manner of the Raiders. They were crouched down in various positions around the farmhouse, some behind a corral, a couple more behind a nearby barn.

Hezekiah jerked out, "Looks like maybe six-seven of 'em. Just a party split off from the main group and gone lookin' for an easy mark. But judging from that gunsmoke coming from Slade's direction in the house they have got a tiger by the tail."

He ran his eye over the whole situation. He snapped, "They ain't seen us yet, Tommy. Let's get up behind them and pepper them some."

They took a wide detour, hidden by an outbreak of brush some distance behind the farmhouse and walked the horses in closer. Dismounting they tied their mounts, Hezekiah's pinto and Tommy's stocky little dun behind them and went on on foot, rifle and scattergun taken from their saddle boots in hand.

Hezekiah said, "Here's where we give them hell-raising, throat-cutting killers a little surprise." He sighted along the barrel of his rifle with his eye and squeezed the trigger with his left forefinger. A raider, shot through the back of the head, fell forward as if he had just dozed off.

At the same moment Tommy's shotgun boomed. Another raider in the very act of firing his carbine at the farmhouse let out a cry of pain and dropped the gun from a shattered right shoulder.

Both Hezekiah and the deputy began pumping lead as fast as their trigger fingers could work. At the sound of the new barrage Slade's firing from the house seemed to gain new vigour.

The raiders, totally surprised and unaware of the size of the force now behind them, started running for their horses. They leapt into their saddles and headed away at full gallop from the combined fire of Slade and the two lawmen. As one of them drew further away he stood up in the stirrups and looked back. The sunlight flashed like fire off a great knife he slashed through the air in the direction of the two lawmen. With a lightning movement he passed the blunt side of the blade across his throat in a threatening gesture. Then with a defiant roar he galloped off.

Hezekiah came out of the brush with the deputy and stared after the departing raiders. "That," he said flatly, "was Big Knife Benito, Tommy, I think we just saved John Slade's head from parting company with his shoulders."

They went back for the horses and trotted up to the house. John Slade came out to meet them, smoke still drifting from the muzzle of his hot rifle.

Hezekiah said amiably, "John, you still fixing to keep running your farm with these varmints closing in closer every day?"

Slade shook his head. "Looks like you're right, sheriff. Guess I'll have to do what others are doing. Forget about my crops and bring my stock in closer to the town, maybe right into town. Maybe have to corral them, feed them on hay, water them from troughs. But how long can a thing like that last?"

Hezekiah squinted his eye. "Depends on just how long Romero sets up a siege." Slade offered, "Or is kept out." He stared unblinkingly at the sheriff.

"And just how long do you think he can be kept out?"

Hezekiah pondered a moment. "Don't know. All I know is we've got to look to the army for help and every manjack in town has got to be prepared to fight as fierce as ole Beelzebub himself to keep the raiders out."

John Slade looked around at his farm. He said bitterly, "Don't see why I've got to leave all this to fall into the hands of a bloodthirsty greaser who dresses up fancy and sees himself as the next president of Mexico."

Tommy Turner spat on the ground. "Finish up he'll get nowhere fast. Them greasers change their presidents faster than womenfolk change their minds."

"And meantime," said Slade gloomily, "we have got to do as best we can while these murderin' cut-throats ride like crazy men over our land."

"Over Romero's land," corrected Hezekiah. "That's what he figures it is."

He looked across at a corral where

a few fine head of horses were milling around, still disturbed by the gunfire. "Lucky you didn't get them run off, John. Maybe if you're gunna start shifting things we oughta give you a hand right now to move those good-lookin' mustangs somewheres safer."

John Slade nodded and began to walk towards the barn to get a saddle for one of the horses he would ride. Tommy Turner grumbled, "Bad day when we gotta run away from these mangy coyotes."

Hezekiah said, "Come on, we got work to do."

★ ★ ★

Back in Davenport after having seen John Slade's horses taken care of, Hezekiah set out on a tour of the town, calling in on community leaders, storekeepers and owners of hotels and saloons. He explained to Shane Wartman, owner of the town's best hotel, "I'm sending to a couple of the nearest army outposts for whatever troopers they can spare. I have a feelin' it just might get to be their problem pretty soon."

The well-dressed hotel-keeper in the fancy vest and striped trousers flicked the ash off his cigar and asked doubtfully, "Is this a genuine threat, Hezekiah? To run off some cattle and horses from ranches and farms, even to kill a few people is one thing, but to take on a whole town — "

The sheriff said carefully, "If I was a gamblin' man and had a pokeful of gold dust I would bet it, my horse and my gun on Luis Romero doing exactly what he has given every clear sign of attemptin' to do — to run every American off all the land that he claims is Mexican territory by right. And if we ain't prepared to go — which he knows we ain't — he figures the only way is to drown us in our own blood."

Shane Wartman blinked. "I have a rifle and a Colt .44 if they might be needed but really — "

Hezekiah made to move on to make his next call. "Check 'em both over, Shane. Make sure they're in good working order and stuff 'em full of cartridges. You'll need 'em."

In Henry Porter's store the skinny proprietor with the battered spectacles protested, "Well, now, looky here, I ain't no fightin' man, Hezekiah. Never done much huntin' and besides my eyes ain't too good — "

The sheriff patted his arm. "You got a gun, Henry?"

"Well, yeah, who ain't? An ole blunderbuss my daddy handed on to me. Kicks like a mule." He rubbed a skinny shoulder in painful memory.

Hezekiah said solemnly, "You look like gettin' a mite bruised again, Henry, but we're gunna need your gun."

Down further along the boardwalk the bulky Widow Wilson stormed up to the sheriff. "Hezekiah Horn, what is this thing you are running around telling the whole town about? This cock-and-bull story about Davenport

211

being besieged?"

Hezekiah said patiently, "If you'll notice, Rebecca, I ain't been runnin'. Got a gimpy leg that don't take kindly to that. But what I've been tellin' people is as true as that the sun will rise in the east tomorrow and set in the west unless, the Almighty is plannin' to change things around a bit. We are going to be attacked by a horde of bloodthirsty Mexicans."

The big woman sniffed loudly, "They had better not try it but if they do I've got a gun that will blow them to Kingdom Come. My first dear departed husband was a buffalo hunter and I can use that weapon as good as he did."

Hezekiah gave her one of his occasional grins. "Good for you, Rebecca. I got no doubt you will pepper those varmints. Never been no truer weapon than that gun of yours with its drop block action. Keep it handy, gal."

He kept going on his calls. The town had to be prepared and his message was getting through.

14

Gun Thunder

TOMMY TURNER came galloping in, the fastest Hezekiah had ever seen him move the little dun gelding. Through the window of his office Hezekiah watched the little man pull his sweating mount to a halt and climb down from the saddle. The sheriff thought, little and old as he was there was no better scout around. Seemed like the deputy had something important to tell him.

Tommy came through the door with a clump of fast-moving feet. He scowled at the sheriff, "You better git them fort-tee-fications in place right smart. If that Romero and his raiders ain't fixin' right now to head for this town with war on their mind then I am a long-necked turkey gobbler."

Hezekiah nodded, getting to his feet. "You see Apache Joe?"

"Sure did." The deputy's scowl grew deeper. "But lemme tell you he don't look a pitcher of rosy-cheeked health as yet. An' also he's having some trouble talkin' some of his bronco braves into joinin' up with us. But, one thing, he's got the shaman backin' him up."

Hezekiah, heading for the door, turned back. "That's good. That old man has a lot of sway with that tribe." He gave his occasional fleeting grin. "The old feller sprinkle you with his magic dust so that bullets will bounce off you?"

"Tell you somethin', sheriff," growled Tommy. "We're gunna need some of that Apache magic before we are through."

"Guess you're right. Meantime get your little dun unsaddled and watered. Looks like he needs a drink bad. And then get up the north end of town and see the folks start putting up the barricades. I'll take the south end."

Hezekiah limped off, heading up the main street, putting his head into doorways and calling out, motioning to passers-by in the street, stopping here and there to talk urgently to both men and women.

People began moving about quickly. At the south end of town soon there was piled up right across the street a motley collection of over-turned buckboards, barrels, logs, sacks filled with sand, anything that would help to provide a defensive wall. The pile mounted higher into a barrier of considerable strength.

Hezekiah looked up the other end of town. Directed by Tommy the same thing was happening up there. The sheriff turned to Shane Wartman who was standing by, looking disbelievingly at what was happening. "Shane, watch that this barricade keeps gettin' put up, will you? I wanna talk with Tommy."

The hotel-keeper moved out on the street, shaking his head. "This could be a heap of foolishness, Hezekiah." The sheriff said flatly, "Better to be foolish than dead." He moved off to pick up the deputy. Tommy saw him and came to meet him. Hezekiah asked, "What's the size of Romero's force and what time do you figure he'll get here?"

The deputy squinted his eyes. "Got a good look at 'em through my tellyscope from the top of a canyon I found 'em camped in. Hezekiah, that Mex raider got a whole army. He's been pickin' up new followers all over. A lot of rurales have joined him. It's like he was that one they talk about in that Good Book you're always readin' — the Mess — somethin' or other — "

Hezekiah prompted, "The Messiah?"

Tommy nodded. "Yeah. A Messiah come to lead 'em to a Promised Land. I tell you, Hezekiah, I don't scare easy but a look at that horde — "

"H'm." Hezekiah turned away again. "Get the ammo out at your end. I'll attend to mine. I figure they'll hit us from the south end first. When they do, keep a small force up your end just in case some of the raiders double back up that end but send the main body of your people down my end. We want to have as much concentrated fire power as we can get. That was a policy of Napoleon Bonaparte. Don't spread your fire too wide. Concentrate on a point where it will do most harm."

Tommy grunted, "You git them two riders off to the forts?" Hezekiah nodded. "Yup. One north to Fort Sheridan, one east to Fort Bayliss. Sent that fat cowboy, Charley Hicks, one way and a bartender from one of the saloons who offered to go on the other."

He frowned. "Wish Charley would have picked another horse than that big white gelding of his. See it miles off. And that barkeep was wearin' a red shirt that showed up like a prairie fire. But they laughed when I told them they looked too conspicuous. Anyway, let's hope they get back with some troops."

People were pouring out into the street now, moving to the barricades at either end, men as marksmen, women to reload the guns. Ammunition was carted out in boxes and weapons were on full display. Hezekiah moved around, advising, directing, encouraging. He saw someone with a shotgun and approved. "Hey, that's a choke bore. Fine new gun. Can't miss with that at close range."

A bewhiskered old fellow came past trailing a weapon with a mile-long barrel. Hezekiah smiled. A Kentucky rifle. "Get a raider in your sights at a hundred yards, pa, and he'll be a dead 'un."

The Widow Wilson had joined the men as a shooter, carrying a big heavy gun. She said loudly, "I need a tripod for this Sharps. Carries the shot further. Only trouble is got to stand up to shoot it that way."

Hezekiah cautioned, "Better not stand up, Rebecca. There's a lot of you they couldn't miss." The widow bridled, "You commenting on my bulk, sheriff?" Hezekiah gave his once in a while smile. "No, Rebecca, only on your true grit." He kept on moving around, talking, boosting, backing up, offering suggestions.

It was perhaps three hours later that the first horsemen came into view. They came up from the south end of the street, lined up as if to make a cavalry charge, six abreast, line after line.

Shane Wartman, holding a rifle as if it was a foolish thing to do, stared, mouth agape. "My God, you were right — " Hezekiah nearby said drily, "He generally is." Someone, tensed-up and nervous, fired the first shot from behind the barricade.

One of the raider horsemen yelped and grabbed an arm, blood beginning to soak the white sleeve. In a moment the riders wheeled their horses and dismounted, whipping carbines out of their saddle boots as they left the backs of their mounts.

Hezekiah could hear a voice barking orders. Romero, he figured. The riders scattered, taking what cover they could find and Romero's voice was heard again. Instantly there began a fusillade of deadly fire, ordered and co-ordinated, unending streams of lead being poured into the barricade. Hezekiah went flat on the ground, yelling at all the other defenders to get down.

The withering fire kept up, drenching the air with lead, splinters of wood, driven by the bullets, flying from the barricade in showers. It seemed as if the whole world had become one unceasing roar of gunfire. Hezekiah thought quickly, it's like the devastating Union artillery fire at Gettysburg. When the ears seemingly couldn't stand it any longer, it suddenly stopped.

Hezekiah looked quickly up and down the line of defenders. The old fellow with the Kentucky rifle had never fired it. He was lying there, a raider's bullet through his head, just as if he had dozed off in his rocking chair. There was a woman hastily binding up the bleeding arm of her husband.

A boy, hardly into his teens, had crept out with a gun and had dropped it in fear at the furious fusillade and was now crouched over, weeping with shock. At the far end of Hezekiah's left a woman was wailing over a man's still body.

He caught a glimpse of the Widow Wilson crouching down and determinedly reloading her buffalo gun. He nodded at the sight. If she ever corraled Tommy Turner the little deputy might not be getting a looker but certainly a lady with a lot of spunk.

Hezekiah, keeping down low, moved along the line of defenders, talking to each one as he went, supporting, encouraging.

Suddenly there was a stir on the raiders' side. A voice called a greeting in Spanish and there came into view a figure on horseback carrying a white flag.

It was Luis Romero himself, no less impressive in fighting regalia than he was when wearing the elaborate attire of a great patron of the hacienda.

Someone behind the barricade muttered something and raised a rifle but Hezekiah barked out an order not to shoot. The rifle was lowered reluctantly.

Luis Romero, mounted on a great black horse with shining flanks and presenting an awesome figure, rode up to the barricade. He shouted, "Yours is a hopeless task. Throw down your arms. Persistence is useless. A jack-rabbit on the prairie would have more chance against a wolf pack. Surrender and we will be merciful."

Hezekiah, still crouched down, called, "As merciful as you were to those families whose throats you slit? If you want us, Romero, you've got to come in and get us."

Luis Romero stood up in his stirrups. "Is that you, Sheriff One-eye? Stand up so I can see you."

Hezekiah called, "An' get my head blown off? I know that flag of truce don't mean anything to your rifle men if any of us is crazy enough to show ourselves."

Romero was silent a moment and then he called again, "I want to show you something." He reached into one of his saddlebags and, drawing out a small bundle, threw it over the top of the barricade. It was a piece of red cloth that fluttered as it fell.

Romero's voice held a touch of sadistic triumph. "That is the shirt of the rider you sent in the direction of Fort Bayliss."

He turned in the saddle and shouted something to the men behind him. One rode forward leading a big white horse. Romero turned back again to face the barricade. He called contemptuously, "You will recognise the mount of the rider you sent towards Fort Sheridan. Unfortunately, neither of the riders have survived. So, you see, military aid is out of the question."

There was silence from behind the barricade. Hezekiah looked quickly along the line. The face of every defender suddenly had a depressed, almost hopeless appearance. Hezekiah lifted his voice. "Never saw the day when a bunch of Americans couldn't beat the tar out of a pack of lowdown greasers, Romero. Turn your horse and skedaddle back to your troops before someone forgits that's a flag of truce you're holdin' up and puts some lead into your belly."

Romero's contemptuous smile turned to a snarl. He called in fury, "I intended to show mercy but now every last gringo's throat will be cut — man, woman and child." He turned his horse and galloped back to his troops. Almost instantly the same fusillade of rifle fire started up again.

All along the barricade defenders ducked down, every now and then taking a quick snap shot in reply. After a while the firing from the raiders died away. Hezekiah thought, they're going to do that in bursts. Can't keep it up all day. Run out of ammo.

He moved down the line, alerting the defenders, instructing some to fall back and get some rest before taking on night guard duty. As he went down the line suddenly he came across Sheree Brodie. She was armed with a pistol. She said grimly, "This is the gun I took off Myron Merrill. Really belongs to Tommy Turner. But I didn't think your deputy would mind. It's another pistol against Romero."

Hezekiah gave her his very occasional smile. "Good for you, girlie. This town is sure glad you came here." She flashed a grateful smile at him and turned back to looking steadily through a small gap in the barricade.

Further on Hezekiah found John Slade with Rachel Jones beside him keeping a spare gun loaded for the farmer. She smiled apologetically at the sheriff. "I am no marksman but I can at least do this and help any who might get hurt." Hezekiah patted her shoulder. "You're doin' fine, teacher. Just fine."

At the end of the line Hezekiah found himself looking at Emily Anderson. He said quickly, "Now, Emily, there ain't no call for you — "

She said grimly, "There is every call for me to be here, Hezekiah." She patted the weapon in her hand. "Aram taught me how to shoot this. I didn't want to learn but he taught me just the same. And now I'm putting that to some use." She looked at him intently. "Things are not good, are they?"

Hezekiah touched the hook to his chin. "Now, Emily, I would judge that remark to have some real degree of accuracy. Here we are with half an army against us, our two riders going for help waylaid and killed, barricades that if the enemy likes to risk a cavalry charge could be trampled underfoot and a lot of our fighting force women and girls instead of men. We jest ain't holdin' too many aces." He fixed his eye steadily on her. "An awful lot like the Alamo, ain't it?"

Emily smiled at him. "Just as well you're not married to that teacher girl. You use an awful lot of 'ain'ts', don't you, Hezekiah?" The sheriff nodded.

"Well, they were sort of required there, Emily. But let me tell you something. Our throats have not yet been cut and before Romero can lay a knife to any one of them he is going to find himself and his troops bleeding quite a bit."

He leaned forward suddenly and kissed her on the cheek. "An' I'll do my dangedest to make sure that ain't the last time I do that."

She smiled and touched her fingers to his lips. He moved off, very glad she was there. He went back to Slade. "John, you be in charge of the ammo. Make sure it's kept up to everybody in the line."

The farmer asked soberly, "How long's it gunna last us?"

Hezekiah said curtly, "Long enough. We ain't gunna pull the barricade down and let Romero in. He'll have to fight every inch of the way and he's gunna be covered with blood before he gets past us — if ever he does."

He looked up at the sky. Night was starting to come on. He moved about, getting the night guards on duty, warning them about the probably stealthy attacks in the dark. He clipped out, "Slippery as the Apaches, only while the Injuns won't fight at night these critters do."

With nightfall the firing on both sides had stopped apart from an odd shot now and then. Hezekiah sought a spot removed from the barricade and dozed off for an hour.

He woke up to hear the scuffle. A couple of the raiders had wormed their way up to the barricade. John Slade and another man Hezekiah recognised even in the dark as Shane Wartman were wrestling with the raiders.

Hezekiah sped across to them. One raider turned as he heard him come, knife in hand, leaving Wartman. Hezekiah with a chain-lightning movement kicked the knife out of the man's hand and at the same moment Shane Wartman shot the man through the head with his Colt .44. The raider fell almost on top of the sheriff. Hezekiah threw his body off and turned to Slade.

The man the farmer was wrestling with had already slashed Slade across the arm and the wound was showing up, wet and ugly. Sheree Brodie had suddenly appeared, pistol in hand, aiming it at the raider tangling with Slade.

Another raider, unseen by any of them, squirmed up out of the dust, knife in hand. Seeing the girl with pistol cocked he threw the knife. It thudded into Sheree's chest almost to the hilt. As she fell Hezekiah's gun roared from his left hand and the raider who had thrown the knife fell forward on to the barricade, blood pouring from his dying mouth.

Slade with a mighty effort threw off the raider he was struggling with and at the same moment Hezekiah and Shane Wartman blasted the man with two thundering shots.

Slade, bleeding, was already on his knees beside Sheree. He lifted her head but already the death glaze was in her eyes. Her voice came faintly to him. "You and Rachel — if you have a girl child think about calling her Sheree — " Slade lowered her gently to the ground.

15

End of the Day

THERE had been no more activity through the night. With the daylight Hezekiah began stirring all the defenders. He figured the raiders would begin another fusillade as soon as it lightened.

But there was only an odd shot. It seemed that all Romero had firing were his snipers. High noon came and passed and still no sign of attack from the raiders. Late in the afternoon Hezekiah conferred with John Slade, Shane Wartman and Tommy Turner whom he had called down from the barricade at the other end of the town. He said abruptly, "What's his game? What does Romero figure on doing? Starving us out? But if he's gunna go on with his campaign after Davenport he's not gunna help his cause by wasting time."

Tommy Turner growled, "I sorta figure he might be waitin' for somethin', I dunno what."

Hezekiah snapped, "Waitin' for what? He's got all the troops he needs right now to take this town. He ain't waiting on orders from anyone because he is a law to himself."

"Maybe," offered Shane Wartman, "it's a war of nerves he's playing." John Slade added, "Yeah, and knowin' the ways of these Mex raiders he's maybe toyin' with us like a cat playin' with a mouse."

"Yeah," admitted Hezekiah, "could be that but I figure Romero to be a pretty smart tactician and it don't seem good tactics to hang around waitin' when he's really got us on a hook." He looked around at the others. "Well, we better get back to our posts. Don't want him jumpin' us when we ain't ready."

The afternoon wore on and the

evening came. Throughout the day there had only been desultory firing from the raiders, an odd short burst now and again that seemed more to keep the defenders on edge than anything else.

Hezekiah again talked to the other three. He shook his head. "Can't figure it out. Why is he holding back like this?" The others shook their heads in turn. Tommy Turner said doggedly, "I still think he's waitin' for somethin'."

Hezekiah grunted, "Well, whatever it is we've got no way of tellin'. But what we've got to do right now is put on extra night guards. Maybe he's plannin' a mass night attack with Big Knife Benito in the lead."

Shane Wartman shivered a little at the thought. They broke up, a couple to snatch some sleep, the other two to join others on night guard.

Slowly the night wore away but there was no action from the raiders. In the early light Hezekiah was a study in bewilderment. He talked to John Slade,

"Can't make head nor tail of it. It's like you've put on boxin' gloves in a ring and the other feller won't come out of his corner. It's mighty peculiar and it don't smell good."

Slade nodded. "Got me beat, too, Hezekiah." The sheriff moved off to confer with others.

An hour or two later there was a sudden shout from the direction of the raiders. It turned into a frantic gabble of sound, cries of excitement, shouts and yells almost as if they had already conquered the town. The defenders behind the barricade stared at one another, puzzled and uncomprehending.

Suddenly there was another movement from the raiders' position. Luis Romero again emerged on his big black horse, holding the same white flag. John Slade muttered to the sheriff, "Whatever he's askin' us to do, Hezekiah, don't agree to it."

The sheriff gave him a quick glance and then looked back inquiringly in the direction of the lone rider. Romero came up close to the barricade. He shouted, "Sheriff One-eye, are you there?"

Hezekiah called back, "Still here, Romero, an' my one eye can still see you as good as ever."

Romero called, "That is good, senor sheriff, for I have something I would like you to feast that eye of yours upon." He turned back to the raiders behind him and slashed his arm down in a signal. Immediately there was movement in the brush and something, handled by a group of men, rolled into view. It was a huge black steel cylinder mounted on wheels, its great black mouth yawning hideously at them.

Hezekiah breathed, "A cannon . . ." The people behind the barricade stared, dumbfounded. Tommy Turner had been right. This was what Romero had been waiting for.

Romero called again, "I hope you will see how much your resistance is worth. I can destroy your barricade in a matter of minutes and, if you continue to resist, your whole town within an hour. I shall not immediately give the order to fire. I would like to grant you a little time to think it over. If you are then still in the mood to resist, we will commence firing." He returned and rode back to his troops.

Hezekiah kept staring for a moment or two and then he moved to call the others together — Slade, Wartman, Tommy and a few other men dominant in town leadership. He moved them across into one of the stores and looked around at them. Someone said, "Looks like he's got us over a barrel."

A couple of others nodded. Hezekiah cut in fiercely, "You know what he's tellin' us, don't you? Let me in so I can cut all your throats — kids included." Someone protested, "Now, maybe he was only bluffin' about that — "

Hezekiah snapped, "Romero doesn't bluff. But what he does think is that with that big pop-gun out there he can scare us into laying down our arms and coming in and doing whatever he wants with us, including raping our women and girls. That's a favourite past-time with these mangy wolves he calls his raiders."

Someone else tried to offer another protest but Hezekiah held up his steel claw impatiently. "I'm tellin' you what that cut-throat grandee will do if we lie down an' let him do it. Now, what we've gotta do is this. Everyone leave the barricade and come back to get inside the stores, the hotels and saloons. Then when Romero blasts that barricade he'll knock it down but no one will get hurt. As his troops pour in we'll be under cover and they won't. What we'll have to do is pour as much lead into them as we can until they run for cover. Then it'll just be fightin' house to house."

Someone said, "He ain't gunna keep that big gun quiet. He's gunna start aimin' it at our buildings."

Hezekiah said, "You gotta point there but if we keep scattered he's not gunna be able to blast us all at the same time. Besides, his troops will be in the town and he won't want to hit them." He added a little lamely, "An' maybe some of us can get to it and spike that gun."

There was a wall of silence and then suddenly Shane Wartman spoke up. His voice was calm. "Maybe, just maybe, we're all due to meet our Maker soon, out-manned and out-gunned as we are. But if we are let's go out like Americans, like men, not like runaways — let's fight 'em to a standstill!"

John Slade boomed, "Amen, brother!" and waved his gun aloft. Hezekiah looked around at them all. Wartman's short speech had clinched it. The people would continue resisting. He went out with the men to tell the others. The people silently left the barricade and trooped into the buildings.

After a while, watching from one of the stores, Hezekiah saw Romero again come forward on the black horse. He came near to the barricade and called out. There was no answer. He called again and then realised the defenders had vacated their positions. Scowling, he turned and galloped to where the gun stood, its mouth pointed ominously at the barrier. From horseback he gave a sharp order.

The gun crew brought the mouth of the cannon a little lower and sighted it directly at the centre of the barricade. There were some shouted orders, a moment of silence and then a tremendous roar. The centre part of the barricade flew into the air, cartwheels, barrels, bodies of the buckboards blown to pieces.

A great gaping hole appeared in the defence barrier. The gun was loaded and fired again. Another big section of the barricade disappeared in smoke, littering the ground with shattered fragments.

Again the gun spoke with its thundering roar. The barricade was next to demolished. Luis Romero, roused to a war-like frenzy, roared a command and galloped forward on his big black horse, a terrible rider straight out of the Apocalypse. He had a sword in one hand, a glittering gold-mounted thing, obviously a family heirloom.

There was a tremendous drumming of hoofbeats behind him as a big section of the raiders galloped in after him. The thundering cavalry tore across the ground, leaping over the remnants of the destroyed barrier, surging into the town, an irresistible horde.

All the people in the buildings started firing but already the raiders were dismounting and letting their horses run while they sought cover from which to shoot back. They were taking care to remain clear of certain buildings and, looking out, Hezekiah could see the cannon being trundled forward to be pointed at the first building occupied by townspeople.

As they brought the cannon closer the crew quickly reloaded it and prepared to fire. But even as they did there was a shout from their rear and the sound of fresh shooting. The gun crew swung around, startled.

Hezekiah's ears, attuned to such a sound, could hear the scream that he knew was a war cry of the Apaches. Joe had kept his word.

The raiders out in the street had picked up the sound and seemed to be uncertain what to do next. Romero, still on his big horse, had also swung around at the sound. There was heavy fighting back there now and he seemed undecided as to where to direct the troops he had with him in the town. Hezekiah exulted. There was nothing more demoralising to any force than to be caught between two fires.

Romero had made up his mind. He motioned his troops in the town to get their horses and follow him back to deal with the Apaches before they came across his prized possession, the big gun, and either turned it on his own troops or put it out of action. He knew the Apaches could not be a very large force and would probably succumb to the raiders' numbers.

The same thoughts were flashing through Hezekiah's mind. He banged the store door open and moved out on to the boardwalk. Romero was galloping right past the door. As he saw the one-eyed sheriff standing there in a gunman's crouch he yelled and as he came sweeping past made a savage thrust with the sword.

Hezekiah ducked under the blade and slashed with the hook. The steel caught in Romero's jacket and jerked him out of the saddle.

Hezekiah winced with the pain that shot like fire up the length of his arm but already his Colt was in his left hand. Romero crashed to the ground, winded. He made a weak effort to clutch at the pistol holstered at his side but Hezekiah's Colt had already thundered in his face. The grandee with plans of glory sank back, his head a mass of gore.

Hezekiah disengaged the hook and let the body of the raiders' leader drop to the boardwalk. He caught a glimpse of a face ugly as Satan with huge black moustaches and blazing eyes galloping past and as it did its owner thundered a shot at him. The slug spanged off Hezekiah's hook, ricocheting into the wall behind him.

Hezekiah thought, Big Knife Benito. He'll probably take command. Already the sheriff was rousting the townsmen out of their hiding places, yelling at them to get horses and follow him. If they could get there in time they could at least help to even up the forces engaged, the raiders he knew being much superior in numbers to the Apaches.

He had gone straight to his own pinto in the corral near the jail and he quickly saddled and mounted him. As he galloped back up the street, other horsemen beginning to follow, he saw the gun crew around the cannon uncertain of what to do. He could see clearly they were not ordinary raiders. They were artillerymen picked up by

Romero from the Lord knew where, specialists who knew nothing of guerilla fighting.

They quaked at the sight of the sheriff's menacing rifle as he whipped it out of his saddle boot and pointed it at them. Hezekiah was aware of the little dun gelding coming up alongside him with Tommy Turner aboard. The deputy already had his scattergun levelled at the gun crew.

Hezekiah rapped, "Take these hombres down to the hoosegow an' lock 'em up. They'll be the only ones who know how to handle this thing." The deputy nodded and the scared men broke into a shambling run as he headed them back down into the town.

Hezekiah moved on. Up ahead the Apaches were making their presence felt but already some of their saddles had been emptied. The raiders generally were fierce, savage fighters, miles apart from the soldiers of the regular Mexican army who often broke ranks and ran wildly in panic.

And then Hezekiah heard something that made his heart leap. It was the brazen call of an army bugle. He looked over to his right and saw the blue-clad cavalry of the United States army in the distance galloping towards the milling force of embattled Apache warriors and Mexican raiders. The raiders had heard the sound and were already breaking ranks.

A horseman, screaming defiance, hurtled past him, heading towards the other end of the town and escape. It was Big Knife Benito. He leapt his horse over the broken barricade and tore up the main street, heading straight towards Tommy Turner and the captives walking ahead of him.

Tommy turned quickly at the sound of the galloping hoofbeats. Benito, yelling abuse, raced up to him, flashing the big knife. He struck once with it as he passed the deputy, the blade sinking deep into Tommy's left shoulder. Almost as if triggered off by the blow the deputy's shotgun exploded.

Benito swayed in the saddle, his middle cut in half with buckshot. He fell from the horse's back, one foot still caught in the stirrup. The frightened horse, still galloping, dragged him for yards before his foot fell loose and his body came to a halt, as still and quiet as he had rendered scores of others with his deadly knife.

Several of the women left back in the town came running out of one of the buildings to tend to the wounded deputy. As they got him down off his pony Hezekiah smiled as he saw that one of the women was the Widow Wilson. She had grabbed hold of Tommy's scattergun, reloaded it in a flash and she and another woman holding a pistol were herding the captured gun crew on down to the jail, Tommy yelling instructions as they went. Hezekiah thought, the little guy can't be hurt that bad.

Up ahead the U.S. cavalry was sweeping in. The raiders were scattering, running, caught between several fires and totally in disarray. The cavalry and the Apaches took off after them, doing a deadly work on the retreating, leaderless mob.

Hezekiah pulled up. He would leave it to the army and the Indians who owed the raiders a good deal of bloody repayment.

He rode back to the town slowly. Tomorrow would see a different dawn over Davenport.

Later the captain commanding the cavalry talked to Hezekiah and Apache Joe. He nodded at the Indian. "The chief sent word to us at Fort Sheridan about Romero and where he was headed. The colonel detailed me and the troop to come and help out. We're going to keep chasing up these troublemakers. Romero had the sort of dream a lot of would-be dictators have. We're going to do our best to dissuade any others from going down the same trail."

After he was gone, Hezekiah turned to Apache Joe, putting out his hand.

"You were a great scout, Joe, and you're a good chief."

Apache Joe smiled. "You know, Chief One-eye, there's a song in an Apache wedding ceremony that ought to suit us two fine. It goes like this: 'Now for you there is no weather; For one is shelter to the other. Now for you there is no fear; For one is protection to the other.'"

As Hezekiah watched the Indians ride off, Emily came over to him. She nodded at Rachel Jones, tenderly rebandaging John Slade's arm; "There'll be wedding bells for those two soon. Hezekiah raised his eyebrow at her. "And maybe for us?"

Emily smiled and patted his arm. "Who knows?" Hezekiah grinned and wandered off to see how Tommy was making out. The little deputy moved his arm under the wrappings. "That Benito's aim was a little off for once." Hezekiah was thinking of something else. He said aloud, "It's gunna be quiet around here. No Apache uprisings, no

Mexican raiders to trail."

Tommy growled, "There's always someone like Myron Merrill driftin' in." Hezekiah nodded. "I guess you're right." He went out and got back up on Pinto Pete again, holding the reins with his hook and cradling the little dog in his good arm.

He would take a turn around a few square miles of Eden County. It was his territory and he intended to do his best to keep it like it said in the old hymn, when peace like a river should flow.

THE END